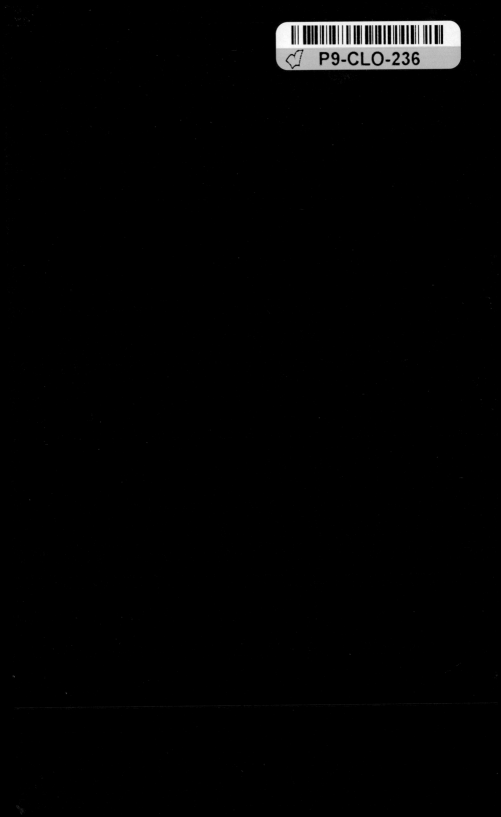

BEFORE THE AWAKENING

WRITTEN BY
GREG RUCKA

ILLUSTRATED BY
PHIL NOTO

PRESS

LOS ANGELES • NEW YORK

For information address Disney • Lucasfilm Press,
1101 Flower Street, Glendale, California 91201.

Printed in the United States of America

First Edition, December 2015

1 3 5 7 9 10 8 6 4 2

FAC-008598-15306

ISBN 978-1-4847-2822-2

Library of Congress Control Number on file

Reinforced binding

Designed by Gegham Vardanyan

Visit the official *Star Wars* website at: www.starwars.com.

SUSTAINABLE FORESTRY INITIATIVE | Certified Sourcing
www.sfiprogram.org
SFI-00993

THIS LABEL APPLIES TO TEXT STOCK

A long time ago in a galaxy far, far away. . . .

A shadow has been cast across the galaxy.
Where once there were hope and peace,
now there are fear and the looming clouds of war.
The FIRST ORDER is rising, its power growing,
and the NEW REPUBLIC may well be powerless to stop it.

Among the billions upon billions of beings in the galaxy,
three individuals will find themselves drawn
into the heart of this conflict.
Each of them will play a vital role in what is to come.
Each of them will face darkness.
Each of them will struggle to reach the light.

FN-2187 is a STORMTROOPER, trained by the First Order.
He is plagued by doubt.
On Jakku, a young woman who calls herself REY
struggles to live in an isolation necessary for her own survival.
And among the stars, POE DAMERON
strives to serve a Republic
he has always believed in, as sinister powers
threaten to break his resolve.

These are their stories in the days, weeks, and months before
THE FORCE AWAKENS.

FINN

THERE WERE four of them in the fire-team, and because shouting out things like, "FN-twenty-one eighty-seven, watch your back!" was a mouthful, especially when the blaster fire was searing the air around them, they'd defaulted to shorter versions. In front of the officers, in front of Captain Phasma especially, they *always* used their appropriate designations, of course. But in the barracks and in combat, they used the names they'd given one another or the names they'd given themselves.

FN-2199, he was Nines, because he liked the sound of it, simple as that. FN-2000 had told everyone to call him Zeroes, because he was proud of the fact that he'd landed such a straight-forward number as his designation. He thought it made him special, and either nobody had ever told him that being a "zero" wasn't exactly something to be proud of or he didn't care.

FN-2003 was the only one with an actual nickname. They called him Slip. He always seemed just a little slower, a little clumsier than the rest of the fire-team. It wasn't simply physical, either. Sometimes—in briefings, during training, during drills—you got the feeling that orders didn't quite take with him, that he didn't, or couldn't, fully understand what it was he was supposed to be doing or how he was supposed to be doing it.

FN-2187 was simply Eight-Seven whenever one of the team wanted to shorten his designation. They didn't do it very often. He was, as far as the training cadre and his peers were concerned, one of the best stormtroopers anyone had ever seen. He was everything their instructors wanted— loyal, dutiful, brave, smart, and strong. Whatever the test, whatever the evaluation, FN-2187 consistently scored in the top 1 percent. So he was FN-2187, well on his way to becoming the ideal First Order stormtrooper. That was what everyone thought, at least.

Except FN-2187 himself.

———

FN-2003—Slip—had fallen behind.

FN-2187, Zeroes, and Nines had taken cover behind what was left of an exterior perimeter wall, the section they were sheltering behind still mostly intact but cracked and scored with innumerable blaster hits. The wall marked the edge of the Republic compound, still heavily defended, and the suppressing fire being directed their way was withering. Bolts of bright blue sizzled overhead and smashed into the ground around them. They punched into the wall with enough force that the stormtroopers could feel the impact even through their armor.

"He did it again," Zeroes said, elbowing FN-2187 and then pointing up-range, the direction from which they'd advanced.

FN-2187 crouched down and looked in the indicated direction. They were all virtually indistinguishable in their stormtrooper armor, but within his helmet, along with the near-constant stream of data projected across his lenses—telemetry, firing solutions, atmospheric conditions, everything up to and including the ammo count for his blaster rifle—individual ID tags would pop up whenever he looked directly at another trooper, his in-suit computer reading friendly identifications. According to that same stream of data, 2187 could see that Slip was exactly 29.3 meters back, crouched in cover behind the hulk of a blasted-out Republic speeder.

He could also see what Slip couldn't—a squad of five Republic soldiers advancing on him unseen from the left flank. FN-2187 raised his rifle, sighting, but he knew before his helmet confirmed it that he was out of range. He could open fire, but there was no way he'd score a hit.

"He's done," Nines said. "We've got to advance."

"He's one of us," 2187 said, lowering his rifle.

"We've got an objective," Zeroes said. He jerked a thumb over his shoulder, toward the base. "It's that way. We go back for him, we'll be cut to shreds."

Face hidden inside his helmet, FN-2187 frowned. Yes, they had an objective, and yes, there were enemies all around them, and yes, Zeroes was right. In the compound was their objective: an enemy position defended by a heavy repeating blaster. And whichever Republic soldiers were manning that thing, they knew their job. They'd seen two full squads cut down by it during their advance. The only reason 2187 could figure it hadn't taken out Slip already was that whoever was on the trigger was waiting to see if one of them was going to do exactly what FN-2187 was thinking of doing—go back for him.

"We're running out of time," Zeroes said.

FN-2187 checked over his shoulder, back toward the compound. The terrain was uneven, and there was enough cover for a sustained fire-and-move advance. It would thin out the farther they advanced into the compound, approaching the heavy blaster emplacement, but it was doable if it was done smart.

"Zeroes, left. Nines, take right," FN-2187 said. "On my order. Hold at the inner wall."

"We're gonna blow the mission," Nines said.

"Hold at the inner wall," 2187 said again. "Go!"

Neither Nines nor Zeroes liked it, 2187 could tell, but they were stormtroopers, and that meant once orders were given they would follow them and follow them quickly. They moved at once, and 2187 waited a half-breath's pause, letting each of them draw enemy fire, before launching forward. The terrain was just as bad in that direction, cruel, uneven, and strewn with broken rock and battle debris. Thick black clouds from engine fires clung to the ground, rolling across it like an uneven tide. He sprinted the first dozen meters, trying to keep low, zigzagging his way from points of cover and occasionally hurdling obstacles in his way.

He'd closed half the distance when one of the Republic soldiers saw him and gave a shout of alarm that carried across the battlefield. Just as the soldier opened fire, FN-2187 dove forward, tumbled into a freshly made crater, and lay flat for a second before popping up on his elbows. He fired twice before dropping down again, then rolled to his right and repeated, firing three times. He was pleased to see that he'd taken out two of the enemy.

But that left three more, and now he had their attention.

FN-2187 keyed his radio. "FN-2003, check right, check left!"

There was static, then Slip's voice. "I don't see them!"

"*Your* left!"

Another blast of static, loud enough that it

made FN-2187 wince. He rolled back to his initial position and edged his way to the lip of the small crater just in time to see Slip opening fire on the remaining Republic soldiers closing in on his position. Now 2187 could take his time. He sighted carefully, then stroked the trigger on his blaster rifle three times in succession. The last of the enemy soldiers dropped.

"On me!" he shouted, but he needn't have bothered, because Slip was already out of cover and running toward him. FN-2187 rolled onto his back, making room in the crater as Slip slid into place next to him and rapped him on the chest plate hard enough that it sounded like he was knocking on a door.

"Thanks, 2187," Slip said. "Thank you, man. Thought you were gonna leave me behind."

"You're one of us." He pointed back the direction he'd come. "Stay tight on me."

"Right behind you."

FN-2187 took another moment to catch his breath, then vaulted out of the crater, Slip clambering up behind him. The fire from the Republic base seemed to have diminished, but FN-2187 knew that was an illusion, that it was just as intense as before, only less concentrated. That, of course, had been his plan: by splitting Zeroes and Nines, he'd forced the enemy to divide their attention, and that had given him the opening he needed to reach Slip. The downside was that Zeroes and Nines were now isolated, pinned down with no way to escape.

But there was a benefit to that, too, 2187 realized. With the enemy fire divided, it gave him a straight shot to the bunker, to the heavy repeater and their objective. All he had to do was be quick and not lose his nerve.

He began running faster. He heard Slip struggling to keep up behind him, but he could no longer worry about that, he realized. If he could do this, if he could do it fast enough, it wouldn't matter if Slip stayed tight on his back or not. If he could do this, not only would he obtain their objective but he might do it without losing anyone on his fire-team.

Another cloud of smoke billowed across his vision, and cutting through it were the red and blue bolts of blaster fire—Zeroes's and Nines's and the enemy's, too. He could hear his breathing, amplified within the helmet, feel his pulse in his temples. The bunker was ahead, the data across his lenses declaring the objective twenty meters away, then fifteen, then ten.

That was when they saw him, but it was already too late. He could see motion inside the bunker, see the Republic soldiers manning the gun react to the sight of him racing toward them and try to swing the barrel around in time. He could imagine himself as they saw him, the immaculate white armor, the symbol of unity and strength and power and skill that was a First Order stormtrooper.

Just before they had their shot, he dropped low, sliding feetfirst toward the edge of the bunker—one hand holding his rifle against his chest, the other going for one of the grenades on his belt. He rolled at the last moment, thumbing the activator hard as he collided sideways with the bunker wall and then, in one smooth motion, bringing his hand up and tossing the grenade through the opening into the bunker. Almost instantly there was the sound and the flash of the explosive detonating. He felt it echo, the vibration running through his armor.

For a moment there was silence, interrupted

only by the sound of FN-2187 trying to catch his breath.

The world flickered, froze, and then winked out of existence. Where there had been an unnamed Republic outpost, where there had been dead stormtroopers and Republic soldiers, there were only four walls and a perfectly flat metal floor. Where there had been a battlefield, there was only the simulation room, vast and empty and cold and sterile. High on one wall, the observation window became visible—heavily tinted, making it impossible to see who was inside.

Then Captain Phasma's voice echoed over hidden speakers.

"Simulation objective completed. FN-2187, FN-2199, FN-2000, FN-2003, report for evaluation and debriefing."

"They completed the objective," General Hux said. "There is that."

"They completed the objective due to the skill of FN-2187's leadership," Captain Phasma said.

They stood side by side at the observation window, watching as the fire-team filed out of the simulation room below. Three of the four were clearly jubilant, clapping one another on the back and shoulders, pleased with their performance. But the fourth—FN-2187, Phasma could tell— was following behind them, not quite part of the group. As she and Hux watched, 2187 paused at the exit, looking back in their direction. Phasma wondered what he was thinking.

"He isolates himself," Hux said, turning to look at her. "A good leader, part of his unit but standing apart."

"If that's why he's doing it, General."

"You have concerns?" Hux raised an eyebrow. "Speak them."

"These stormtroopers will be the finest the First Order has ever produced," Phasma said. "I have overseen their training at every stage, from induction to deployment. This class is exemplary."

"Yet you have concerns, Captain. I would hear them."

"Not for this class."

Hux sighed, at the edge of annoyance.

"FN-2187," Phasma said, "has the potential to be one of the finest stormtroopers I have ever seen."

"From what I just observed, Captain, I agree."

"But his decision to split the fire-team and return for FN-2003 is problematic. It speaks to a potentially . . . dangerous level of empathy. You heard him."

" 'You're one of us'?"

"Yes, sir. While I am entirely in support of unit cohesion, General, a stormtrooper's loyalty must be higher, as you know. It must be to the First Order, not to one's comrades."

Hux glanced back at the window, surveying the empty simulation room.

"I trust you to remove any impurities from the group, Captain," Hux said. "Wherever they may be found."

The briefing room, like every other section of the base where Captain Phasma oversaw their training, was featureless to the point of sterile. That wasn't to say colorless, however. Amid the wide variety of industrial grays, there was always black and, of course, red (though that was reserved primarily for First Order insignia). It was when the helmets came off the stormtroopers-in-training that the real color emerged—in Slip's pale complexion and hazel eyes; in Nines's almost frighteningly blue eyes and red hair; in the scar that had healed along Zeroes's cheek, contrasting lighter against his dark brown skin. In FN-2187's own reflection, caught in those rare moments in front of a mirror preparing for inspection or in the polished surface of the mess hall tables.

In their armor they were all the same, and that was the point, he understood. But he took pleasure in the moments when he could see their variety and diversity—those moments when he could glimpse the people beneath the armor and see them as more than just faceless, nameless soldiers identified by letters and numbers and nothing more.

He didn't know much about life outside of his training, had little in the way of memories of a time before, in fact. What he knew was what he had been taught, and what he had been taught was simple: the First Order stood against the deprivations of the Republic. The First Order brought law to a lawless galaxy. What little he had seen of the galaxy had been filtered through his training, through the eyes of the First Order, but there was no need or even reason to doubt its truth.

Still, he wanted to see it with his own eyes.

He wanted to know what was out there. Like all the others of his cadre, he was waiting for that day when they would first be deployed, when they would take their skills and their training and finally get to apply them in the service of the First Order, at the command of the Supreme Leader. He was waiting for his chance to defend the people of the galaxy against all those who would threaten it.

Those were his thoughts as he sat in the briefing room with Slip and Nines and Zeroes, all of them still in their armor but now with their helmets off, waiting for Captain Phasma to arrive. Slip was nervous, 2187 could see, even if Nines and Zeroes were not. FN-2187 wasn't certain how he should be feeling. He knew, empirically, that he had done well; he had, in fact, been responsible for the successful completion of the simulation. That should've been enough to give him a sense of pride, if not accomplishment. Yet he couldn't shake the feeling that he had somehow made a mistake, had in some way stepped wrong.

The doors slid open with a hiss, and 2187 got to his feet immediately, in unison with the others, all of them fixing their eyes straight ahead and coming to attention. Captain Phasma moved into the room with the same authority and purpose, the same flawless precision, with which she seemed to do everything. Her armor, unlike theirs, was as reflective as a still pond, and as she walked to the front of the room he could see their images bouncing back at them, distorted and curved.

There was no preamble. There never was. Captain Phasma faced them, surveyed them, and then said, "Adequate."

FN-2187 had learned that "adequate" was the closest Captain Phasma would ever get to saying "well done" or "good job."

"FN-2000, you're wasting ammunition," Phasma continued. "Telemetry indicates you expended one hundred and twenty-seven shots, with a hit ratio of less than five to one. You are assigned to the range tomorrow during your second detail. I expect an immediate and marked improvement."

Zeroes drew himself even higher. "Yes, Captain."

The shiny helmet shifted almost imperceptibly to the left. It was another thing that 2187 had noticed about their captain; you never knew exactly who or what she was looking at. He thought it was Slip, but she spoke to Nines, instead.

"FN-2199, biosensors noted your heart rate eight percent above acceptable range, with an additional twenty-second delay in reverting from strong exertion to resting pulse. Your weight is up two percent, without corresponding gain in muscle mass. Your meals are being modified, and you will begin additional physical training tomorrow, second detail."

"Yes, Captain," Nines said.

Phasma didn't move, not even the slightest shift in the angle of her helmet, yet FN-2187 was absolutely positive she was now looking at Slip. She didn't speak. The silence stretched, and as it went on it changed, and FN-2187 could see Slip growing more and more nervous, fighting the urge to say something. Still the silence grew, and then 2187 could feel it, too, found himself silently urging Slip to stay silent, to wait it out, somehow knowing that if Slip should speak it would be a mistake and that another mistake was exactly what Captain Phasma wanted him to make.

At last she said, "FN-2187, your targeting was exemplary. According to the simulation, you fired your weapon only thirty-six times, scoring kills with thirty-five of those. You deployed one explosive, which resulted in the achieving of the objective and another six enemies killed."

Now they could all see her head move as she looked them over in turn.

"All of you should take your example from FN-2187," Captain Phasma said. "You are dismissed. FN-2187, stay."

The others collected their helmets and headed for the door. Slip shot him a last glance before it sealed shut again. FN-2187 remained standing.

"Why did you go back for FN-2003?" Phasma asked.

"He's one of us," FN-2187 said.

"This is not the first time you've helped him. Your instructors have noted multiple occasions where you've been seen assisting him in various duties. Why are you doing this?"

"We're only as strong as our weakest link, Captain."

"I agree."

"Thank you, Captain."

"I want it to stop."

He blinked, surprised. "Captain?"

"We are only as strong as our weakest link, FN-2187. While you believe you are attempting to strengthen that weak link, I assure you that is not what you are actually doing. Rather than fixing the problem, you are allowing it to persist. As a result you are, in fact, weakening the whole. Further, you are weakening *yourself.*"

FN-2187 frowned, brow furrowing. "Captain Phasma, I don't—"

"You have great potential, 2187. You are officer corps material. Your duty is to the First Order above everything. Nothing else comes before that. FN-2003 must stand or fall on his own. If he stands, the Order is strengthened. If he falls, the Order is spared his weakness. Am I understood?"

"Yes, Captain."

"I sense hesitation."

"No, Captain. None."

"Then it will stop."

He swallowed, then nodded. "Yes, Captain."

"Then that is all. You are dismissed."

————

It took a couple of days after his success in the simulation—and the warning from Captain Phasma—for FN-2187 to realize that something had changed. Activity in the base, in their training, seemed on the uptick—a new, quiet urgency pervading everything they did, everything they were expected to do. Instruction seemed suddenly more intense. Their classwork and lectures, which until then had focused primarily on their duties as stormtroopers—on small-unit tactics, weapons maintenance, military structure and integration—gave way to more discussions on particular deployments, stormtrooper specializations, and localized scenarios using named, known locations. For the better part of a week, they studied and were repeatedly tested on different historical battles, many from the Clone Wars, some even earlier.

They were stormtroopers, but they weren't quite, not yet. They were cadets, and as cadets they had additional duties aside from their training. Those duties covered everything from maintaining the armory to performing minor repairs on equipment to quite literally moving equipment from one location to another, often by hand but frequently with the assistance of the heavy-lifter droids, when whatever was to be moved was too big to be moved manually. They mopped the floors. They emptied the trash. They worked in the galley preparing meals.

Free time in which to relax, simply to rest in the barracks or to read First Order–approved literature or watch First Order–approved vids, vanished. There was always something more to do, somewhere else to be, another session in the simulator or more dishes to wash. There was always someone watching their performance, no matter what it was, someone to tell them that they needed to work faster, work harder, that they had to be *better*.

It didn't leave a lot of time to think, and FN-2187 began to wonder if that wasn't the point.

As grueling as their schedule had become, it was Slip who took the worst of it. He had never been the best under pressure, and his mistakes became more common. Under scrutiny, each error was magnified. Minor infractions—a broken plate when they were doing the dishes, a battery pack left on the wrong shelf in the armory, things that could've happened to anyone—were dealt with punitively, and *all* of them were punished, not Slip alone.

Nines and Zeroes made no secret of their growing resentment. Even FN-2187 felt it. He could see Slip struggling, and he would think to help him, to try to ease his burden, even move to do so.

Then he would remember Captain Phasma and would instead turn away.

He didn't like how that made him feel—almost like he was sick, like there was something sitting deep in his stomach that didn't agree with him. It didn't help that FN-2187 couldn't see any indication from anyone else—not from Nines, not from Zeroes—that they felt the same way. He was sure he felt it alone.

He began to wonder if there was something wrong with him.

There were mandatory morale sessions twice a day, when everyone was required to stop what they were doing and direct their attention to the nearest holoprojector to watch a recorded speech from High Command, most often from General Hux himself. Those would be interspersed with news feeds showing the deplorable conditions throughout the Republic: the famines on Ibaar and Adarlon, the brutal suppression of the population of Balamak, the unchecked alien advances throughout the Outer Rim. There would always be at least one story to follow about a First Order victory, the liberation of a labor camp on Iktotch or a fleet battle in the Bormea sector. Everyone would cheer, and FN-2187 noticed that Slip would cheer loudest of all, maybe because he was having such a hard time with everything else.

For his own part, FN-2187 didn't much care for the morale sessions, seeing them mostly as a waste of time that could be better spent in other ways. They were all First Order, after all; it wasn't like anyone could forget who they were or what they were fighting for. He would applaud when he was supposed to applaud and chant when he was supposed to chant and cheer when it was right to cheer. But his heart wasn't in it, and he wondered if he was alone in that, too. Perhaps Nines or Zeroes felt the same way. He wanted to ask them but found he was afraid to. What if they didn't? What if he really was the only one who felt that way?

———

"I can't wait to get into combat," Zeroes said.

They were in the mess hall, all of them rushing to clean their plates. Everything in their day was regimented, an allotted number of minutes for bathing, for dressing, for training, for eating. If you went over on time, someone would come along and take your plate as you were trying to finish. All of them had learned to eat quickly or else go hungry. The result was that if you tried to talk and eat at the same time, you'd end up failing at both. Zeroes's comment was therefore something of a surprise.

Nines laughed. "You've got numian cream all over your chin, Zeroes. Don't let Captain Phasma see you like that."

Zeroes wiped at the mess with the back of his hand, then leaned forward over his plate. "It's coming, you can feel it. No more exercises. An actual deployment."

FN-2187 looked at him, curious. "You know something we don't?"

"I heard some of the instruction officers talking."

This got all their attention.

"Saying what?" asked Slip.

"They're accelerating our training. They say we have to be ready."

"Makes sense." FN-2187 used the corner of a chunk of mealbread to wipe up the last of the cream on his plate. The meal, like so many others, hadn't been designed for flavor as much as efficiency—slivers of overcooked meat in a numian sauce that tasted more like chalk than anything else. But it was filling and provided energy, and that was the point.

"I hope it's soon," Slip said. "I really hope it's soon."

"Don't hope it's too soon." Nines drained his glass, then set it down hard and stared at Slip. "Way you're going, your first deployment might be your last."

"Hey," FN-2187 said. "He's one of us. We're in this together."

Nines and Zeroes exchanged looks.

"Yeah?" Zeroes said. "Well, way he's going, I'd rather it be just the three of us."

The look on Slip's face said it all—said more, actually, made FN-2187 wonder if he didn't have doubts, too.

Maybe FN-2187 wasn't alone in what he was feeling after all.

Whatever the reasons for it, whether Zeroes could be believed or not, their training *did* accelerate. They were in the simulators two, three times a day, sometimes running combat missions as a single fire-team, sometimes working in concert with the other members of a larger squad. Twice they participated in multiforce battles, base assaults where their simulator was tied to the action in fifty others, all of them running at the same time. They were massive engagements, with full air support, advancing armor, even orbital bombardment from capital ships. TIEs screamed overhead, engaging Republic X-wings in dogfights that streaked through the simulated skies.

FN-2187 found himself actually enjoying those simulations, so much so it almost surprised him. The simulations were simple. The stormtroopers had a clear objective, they knew who the enemy was, and honestly, as serious as the simulations could be, they were ultimately just games, ones he knew he played well. In that kind of environment, it was easier to heed Captain Phasma's advice, to let Slip rise or fall on his own. When Slip went down—and he always went down—it didn't really matter, because none of it was real, was it?

After the second multiforce battle simulation, Captain Phasma singled out FN-2187 for praise in front of everyone who had participated. She had him stand and face the debriefing—and there were hundreds of them there that time, all the pilots and stormtroopers and instructors; it felt like everyone. She talked about his skill and his efficiency and his ruthlessness, how all the trainees could learn something from watching FN-2187. It made him feel awkward, even embarrassed, and he was thankful he had his helmet on so no one could see him.

The following morning they started on intensive melee combat training. This was done outside the simulators, in one of the exercise rooms designated for the purpose. Previously, FN-2187 and the others had trained in hand-to-hand combat, working in close quarters with fists and feet. This time they found the room prepared with racks of weapons and shields lining the walls.

The instructors demonstrated the use of each weapon, the vibro-axes and shock staffs and force pikes and resonator maces, elaborating at length on the respective strengths and weaknesses of each and when and how to employ them to best effect. They explained the composite alloys used to make the weapons, how some of the equipment was strong enough to block even a lightsaber. FN-2187 wondered about that—not whether it was true but whether or not they would ever be expected to fight someone who used a lightsaber. According to the First Order, the Jedi were extinct.

Soon enough, the instructors passed out the weapons. FN-2187 found himself with a mace and shield. Zeroes and Slip each ended up with force pikes. Nines used a one-handed vibro-axe and a shield. They were told that all the powered weapons carried only a nominal charge, making them incapable of penetrating stormtrooper armor.

They began drills, basic moves—stance, attack, parry—and then repeated, over and over again, until FN-2187 could feel perspiration running down his back inside the bodysuit he wore beneath his armor. When they'd finished, his arms ached from the effort of maintaining the mace and shield, but there was a sense of pleasure, too, the delight of learning something new and learning it quickly and well.

The following morning they resumed the training where they'd left off but now with the introduction of sparring. The instructors would pick two of the trainees to square off against each other. They'd give a go signal, and then it would be on, weapons swinging through the air while the white-armored figures collided, blocking and jabbing and parrying until one was knocked off his feet or one of the instructors announced a winner. The losing combatant would return to the others waiting their turns at the edges of the room, the winner would remain, and it would start again.

FN-2187 realized that, powered or not, armored or not, their weapons could cause real damage. Twice, trainees had to be helped off the floor, one with broken fingers from a particularly savage mace blow, the other stabbed by the tip of a force pike that had slipped off of an armor plate and punctured the membrane holding the plates together.

Slip was the first of their cadre to be called onto the floor, and for a moment while he watched his friend sparring, FN-2187 thought that might be the one thing at which Slip excelled. His footwork was consistent and good, and he kept his force pike in its proper grip. He didn't make any of the obvious mistakes.

It didn't last.

Slip's opponent was using a pike of his own. They were exchanging blows for the sixth time, quick end to end as if fighting with staffs, when suddenly Slip's opponent stepped back, spinning his pike in both hands over his head, then bore down with a blow that cracked so loud on the top of Slip's helmet it sounded like his helmet—and his head—had been split in two. Slip staggered, and his opponent flipped the staff and brought the opposite end up, just as hard, smashing it into Slip's chin. Slip dropped like a stone, and when the instructors removed his helmet, FN-2187 could see blood coming from his mouth, his vision looking unfocused.

Slip got back in line.

The person who remained longest on the floor was Zeroes. He went four bouts without falling, and then FN-2187 was called and ended his run. The force pike gave Zeroes reach and he went in strong, but FN-2187 had his shield and he quickly discovered that, when he angled it properly, he could redirect a jab in almost any direction he wanted. Zeroes tried attacking four times—low, low, low, and then high, driving the pike with both hands toward FN-2187's heart. FN-2187 blocked, angling the shield to his right so that when the blow glanced off, Zeroes was off balance and overextended. FN-2187 spun on his toes in the opposite direction, brought the mace in his other hand around low, and caught Zeroes just above the knee, sending him sprawling.

"Win!" shouted one of the instructors.

FN-2187 moved to help Zeroes back to his feet, dropping his mace and taking him by the elbow. Zeroes shrugged him off, his anger evident even behind his armor. FN-2187 figured that was because he'd broken Zeroes's streak.

It was the start of FN-2187's own streak, however. The next trainee to go at him was from a different cadre, the FO group, also armed with a mace and shield. The fight lasted three seconds. FN-2187 feinted an overhead blow with the mace, and when his opponent brought his shield up to parry it, he hit him instead with his own shield and knocked him flat. His next two opponents were also FO designations, another with a force pike and one with a shield and sword. The second of those took the longest, almost a full minute, before FN-2187 managed to knock away his opponent's shield, and then it was a simple matter of waiting for an opening and striking at the right time.

Then it was Nines's turn, with his vibro-axe and shield, and if FN-2187 had thought Zeroes was angry when he'd lost, Nines seemed to start out that way. Nines began with a swipe straight at FN-2187's head, and the next thing 2187 knew Nines had rammed into him, body to body, their armor clattering as he was pushed back along the training floor. It took all his strength to keep his feet, to keep from giving Nines another opening with his axe, and finally FN-2187 dropped his shield altogether and used his free hand to take control of Nines's wrist. They spun in place, and FN-2187 slammed his shoulder into Nines's chest, sending him off balance long enough to create distance between them. Before he could recover his discarded shield, though, Nines was launching at him again, and FN-2187 was using his mace with both hands, knocking away Nines's attacks as quickly as they came. He could feel his heart pounding inside the armor, the echo of his breathing as it grew labored. The thought occurred to him, unexpected and shocking, that Nines thought this was *real*, not an exercise, not training.

The vibro-axe fell again, slashing at his arm, and FN-2187 skipped back. The two of them began to circle. Nines feinted with the axe, then swung the shield and nearly caught him in the side, but FN-2187 managed to get the mace up to parry just in time. He saw the follow-up coming before Nines launched it, knew the axe was slashing in again, and that time, instead of stepping away from it, FN-2187 stepped *forward* and under Nines's guard. The mace was in the wrong position, its heavy head toward the floor, so FN-2187 used its pommel instead, smashing it into Nines's helmet. The other trooper went sailing onto his back. He laid still, dazed for a moment.

FN-2187 recovered his shield and reset it on his arm. He didn't move to help Nines up.

That was four of them, which tied him with Zeroes's streak.

Bout five was Slip, and right away FN-2187 could see something was wrong. Maybe it was the blow to the head, or something else, but he was moving slowly. His footwork, impeccable before, was sluggish and sloppy. His grip on his force pike kept slipping, not obviously but enough that the point was too low, so it would be easy for FN-2187 to knock it out of the way or even disarm him entirely. In his helmet, tasting his sweat, FN-2187 glanced over at the instructors observing them, looking for any sign that they were seeing what he was, that Slip wasn't up to it, that it wasn't going to be a fair fight at all. The instructors were impassive, standing in their uniforms, hands behind their backs. Nothing in their expressions betrayed anything but vague interest. There was no sign of sympathy.

Slip lunged, and FN-2187 blocked him easily, sending the tip of the pike off his shield and to the left. Slip followed, unable to stop himself in time, almost at full reach and obviously off balance. FN-2187 stepped back, giving him room to recover. Again he glanced at the instructors. One of them, he thought, was frowning.

FN-2187 swung his mace in an easy arc, putting no real power behind it, all but telegraphing the move. Slip barely got his parry in place in time and failed entirely to launch a riposte. They circled. Another glance at the instructors, and both were frowning. Slip tried to flip his grip on the pike and made a staff-end swing that FN-2187 ducked before he'd even thought about it. He had another opening and almost took it but for some reason found himself unable to.

It struck him, then, that if he were to lose, Slip would be left to face whoever went next.

It struck him, too, that whoever Slip fought next wouldn't care that he was already hurt, that another injury might be too much for him.

You're one of us, FN-2187 thought.

He attacked with the mace, an upswing that Slip blocked but without any strength behind it. The parry blew through Slip's guard and sent his hands and the pike high, almost over his head, leaving his middle exposed. FN-2187 stepped forward, leading with his shield, pressing rather than striking while at the same time bringing his left leg forward, behind Slip's right. It took almost no discernible pressure; suddenly, Slip was on his back and FN-2187 was standing over him, and the instructor was shouting.

"Win!"

That was when FN-2187 saw the chrome

reflection, the kick of light off polished armor, and realized that Captain Phasma was watching them.

He stepped back, waiting as Slip pulled himself unsteadily to his feet.

The next combatant was from another training cadre, FL, but FN-2187 didn't really notice and didn't much care. He felt certain Phasma was watching him, though it was impossible to be sure. The FL trainee was using two weapons, a sword and an axe, and he was wild with both. By that point FN-2187's mind was racing—thinking about Slip and Nines and Zeroes, and Phasma watching him—and it wasn't really a surprise when the world burst into a flare of white, when the hilt of the sword connected with his jaw, when he could taste his own blood. One moment he was up, the next he was on his back, staring at the lights in the ceiling through the lenses of his helmet.

He got up and took his place in line.

"I have one question for you, FN-2187."

"Yes, Captain."

"Were you toying with FN-2003? Was that what I saw?"

FN-2187 hesitated, and just doing that, he knew, made Captain Phasma unhappy. If she was angry, he couldn't tell. Through her helmet, her voice was always carefully modulated.

"FN-2003 had been injured in a previous bout," he said. "I didn't want to see him hurt any further."

"I see." Her helmet turned toward him, hidden eyes seeking his, and suddenly FN-2187 felt horribly exposed standing in the briefing room in his armor, with his helmet tucked under his arm, just the two of them. "You didn't want him fighting someone else, someone who wasn't . . . sympathetic to his situation."

"No, Captain."

"Your objective was simple, FN-2187."

"I won the bout, Captain."

"But you considered losing to him first, didn't you?"

FN-2187 didn't respond.

"A real stormtrooper has no room for sympathy," Phasma told him. "A real stormtrooper is the extension of the First Order, of Supreme Leader Snoke's will, nothing less. Do you think the Supreme Leader would have hesitated, FN-2187?"

"No, Captain."

"Gather your fire-team," Phasma said. "You are being deployed."

They moved from the base to a transport and from the transport to orbit, traveling with another half dozen of the trainee squads, all of them in their armor and with their rifles. The rifles were new, no longer the training version but the real thing, F-11D blaster rifles, loaded with live ammunition and fully charged for battle. Their first look at the Star Destroyer, majestic and ominous at once, was through the hull windows as it came into view—almost impossibly small at first, then growing to become almost impossibly large as their shuttle sped toward it.

"This is for real," Nines said, and FN-2187 thought there was awe in his voice, as if he'd never expected them to make it that far.

"Did the captain say where we're going?" Slip asked. "What we're doing?"

"No," FN-2187 replied.

"Of course not," Zeroes said. "She's not going to tell stormtroopers the Supreme Leader's plans, or General Hux's, or even her own. She's not asking for our opinion. She's got a job she wants done and she's counting on us to do it."

They docked in the primary bay and disembarked in tight formation, marching as they had been taught. Ranks of TIE/fo fighters hung on their moorings overhead, gleaming in the docking bay light, and FN-2187 had to work hard not to stare at them, the real things up close. He knew, intuitively, that there was no appreciable difference between the fighters hanging above him and the ones he'd seen fly overhead so many times in simulations, and yet this was strangely, sharply different. Their power was palpable, even ominous, as they waited above like a flock of sleeping, savage mynocks.

The deck officer, an older man in a perfectly tailored, immaculate uniform, was waiting for them. He separated them by cadre and gave them directions to their billets, and FN-2187 found that he and the rest of the team had been assigned to barracks almost identical to those they'd left behind on the surface. The difference was that the ones aboard the ship were occupied by "real" stormtroopers, men who ignored them entirely as they located their bunks and stowed their gear. They'd hardly had a moment to remove their helmets and settle themselves when they heard the order coming over the ship's PA system: all hands prepare for hyperspace. And it wasn't a minute after that when FN-2187 felt the ship shudder slightly and they were off and traveling faster than light.

"Fresh meat," one of the stormtroopers said. "Who's who?"

Slip grinned and indicated himself, then the others. "FN Corps. Slip, Zeroes, Nines, and FN-2187."

"Let me guess," the trooper said. "FN-2187 is in charge, right?"

"That's right."

The stormtrooper fixed FN-2187 with a stare. "No nickname. You're one of those."

"One of those what?" FN-2187 asked.

The stormtrooper laughed. He looked to be in his late twenties, perhaps, but there was something hard in his eyes, and the laugh wasn't amused. "An outsider, cadet. You're on the outside, and you'll always be looking in and wondering why you don't belong."

The rest of the stormtroopers laughed, Nines and Zeroes and even Slip along with them.

———

The deployment was to a mining colony established in an artificial asteroid field collectively known as Pressy's Tumble. Once there'd been an ore-rich moon, but the ore itself had been buried deep, and instead of setting up operations on the surface and sinking mines, some engineer with a facility for explosives had decided the best solution was just to blow the whole thing to smithereens. Those smithereens now floated in the Outer Rim system of Pressylla, along with three inhospitable planets and a red dwarf sun that made the fragments of the lost moon glow with a hellish light.

The largest of the fragments was the base of the mining operation, a sprawling refinery complex that covered most of the surface and had been sunk deep into the rock itself. FN-2187 wasn't exactly sure what was being mined; opinions varied. Some of the stormtroopers said it was fuel, vital to First Order fleet operations. Others said it was some kind of ore needed for starship shield generators. One stormtrooper claimed it was Tibanna gas, but he was clearly mistaken.

What FN-2187 *did* know was that they were there to "restore order," according to the briefing given by Captain Phasma herself. Republic agents, she told them, had infiltrated the mining operations and were both sabotaging equipment and creating dissent among the miners. The First Order's presence was required to put a stop to it, to get the miners back on schedule, and to prevent any further delays.

Theirs was the second squad to shuttle in, and it was different from their trip to the Star Destroyer. This time FN-2187, Slip, Zeroes, and Nines stood in deployment formation for the entire ride, along with another three fire-teams of stormtroopers, some cadets and some more seasoned veterans. All of them were locked and loaded, carrying live ammunition and grenades, and one of the fire-teams, FN-2187 saw, had shock staffs and neurocage nets—weapons designed for crowd control, meant to subdue rather than kill.

They set down within the main facility, the ramp lowering almost before they'd come to a stop. There was a concern they might meet with resistance—rioting or even saboteurs—upon arrival, and for that reason it was a combat exit, all the stormtroopers disembarking in rapid succession, rifles at the ready. They performed the maneuver flawlessly, exactly as FN-2187 and the others had done a hundred times before in the simulators, emerging into a vast loading bay already occupied by one other First Order transporter. The ceiling rose almost fifty meters above them, cut into the rock and braced with scaffolding that dripped rusty water, creating brackish puddles of red and green across the floor. Ten-meter-long artificial lights hung from the braces, flickering irregularly. Beneath his feet, FN-2187 could feel a dull vibration, what he imagined were the drills working the rock far below. Aside from a handful of maintenance droids in the bay, there was no sign of anyone.

One of the veterans, a sergeant, ordered FN-2187 to take his fire-team up to the entrance of the bay and secure it. FN-2187 put Zeroes on point and followed in second position, with Slip behind him and Nines at their backs. The doors were enormous, rising almost as high as the ceiling, and they ground as they pulled open. A wall of noise poured into the bay—the sounds of innumerable machines working, what FN-2187 thought must be the refinery itself.

The bay opened into an enormous cavern,

easily a dozen kilometers across and deeper than he could see. Puffs of steam and green-tinged smoke rose from below, billowing up like the breath of some hidden, sleeping beast. More condensation ran down the walls. It flowed in steady streams, dripping like a lazy rainfall. Worker droids floated across the vast space on repulsorlifts, bobbing and ducking around giant rickety works of scaffolding. Narrow girder bridges linked different levels, some of them at angles that seemed impossible to negotiate without plummeting to one's death. Platforms jutted from the cavern's sides, as unstable-looking as the bridges and supports, many of them draped with tarps.

On one of them, almost directly to his right, FN-2187 saw movement and pivoted, bringing his rifle up in time to catch sight of two humanoids peeking out at them. One was a Talz, the other a Gran. He saw them for only a second before they ducked out of view again, but it was long enough. The Talz was emaciated, tall and scrawny, with missing patches of hair along his arms and shoulders that revealed raw, chalky, peeling skin. The Gran was heavily scarred, what FN-2187 thought was the result of burns, perhaps chemical.

Now that he had seen them, FN-2187 could see others. Almost all the miners were aliens, as varied a mix as the galaxy could offer. Yet to the last of them they appeared malnourished and sickly, many obviously injured. Most wouldn't even glance at the stormtroopers, and the few who did just as quickly looked away again. FN-2187 knew why, and he understood that they weren't just frightened; they were *terrified*.

He felt something in his stomach tighten, then surge. For an instant, he thought he might be sick in his helmet.

They'd been holding position at the entrance of the bay for almost three hours when FN-2187's radio clicked on in his ear. The bay behind them had long before emptied of stormtroopers, the sergeant leading the rest of the troops out into the facility, and Zeroes, Nines, and Slip had begun complaining about how boring the detail was, how it wasn't fair that they'd been stuck there to guard the transporters.

"FN-2187, respond." It was Phasma's voice.

"FN-2187. Go ahead, Captain."

"I am sending a unit to relieve you. Once they

arrive proceed with your team to level alpha-seven-seven, room ought-three. Confirm."

"Confirmed."

The others were looking at him.

"We're being relieved," FN-2187 told them. "Captain Phasma wants us to move to a different location."

"Anything's got to be better than this," Nines said.

"You could be a miner here," FN-2187 said.

"Don't make me laugh. We're not supposed to laugh when in uniform, remember?"

"I'm not joking."

"They could leave if they wanted to," Slip said.

FN-2187 thought of the empty bay behind them, containing only the two transporters that had taken them and the other stormtroopers there. He didn't say anything.

Their relief arrived, another cadet fireteam, and FN-2187 brought up the map he had downloaded to his in-armor computer so it was projected across his vision. They made their way through the complex, along the more stable perimeter walkway and then to an enormous lift that took them down more than five kilometers before finally shuddering to a stop on level alpha-seven-seven. The doors opened onto a view similar to what they'd left above, only even darker, puddles spreading across the floor deep enough that their boots splashed with each step.

Captain Phasma was waiting for them outside a door marked O-3, a half dozen stormtroopers with her.

"Reporting as ordered," FN-2187 said.

Phasma indicated the closed door, her cloak sliding off her arm as she did so. Green and red reflected off her armor.

"The negotiators are inside," she said. "You and your team will accompany me."

"We're negotiating with the Republic?" The question came without thought, and as soon as he had said it, FN-2187 regretted it, expecting Phasma to rebuke him.

"No, for the striking miners." Phasma turned, hitting the activation plate on the wall and opening the door. She led them inside.

Four humanoids sat at the far side of a rectangular slab of a table, opposite the door. Only one was human, his eyes sunken, half his cheek puffed and shiny from a burn scar. The others were a Rodian missing two of the fingers on his right hand, an Abednedo, and a Narquois. All of them straightened in their seats as Phasma entered and watched as she shut the door behind the stormtroopers.

"Have you considered our requests?" the human asked.

"I have given your request the thought it deserves." Phasma looked at FN-2187 and the rest of the fire-team. "Kill them."

Nothing happened for a moment, no movement, not a word, as if everyone—the negotiators and cadets alike—was unsure of what he'd heard.

Then Slip opened fire.

Then Zeroes, then Nines. FN-2187 raised his rifle to his shoulder, his finger on the trigger, and saw the Abednedo in his sights. He saw his wide eyes and all his fear, and in that instant he saw a life full of suffering that was about to end, and he told himself that perhaps what he was about to do was a mercy. Still he couldn't pull the trigger.

In the end he didn't need to.

Slip did it for him.

There was a simple simulation room aboard the Star Destroyer, and FN-2187 booked time in it almost as soon as they were back aboard. He punched up a basic escalation program, a low-level combat scenario in an urban environment that would gradually increase in difficulty. He checked his weapon and entered the simulation.

At first, it was as easy as it had ever been. The enemy appeared—Republic soldiers in that scenario—the rifle kicked softly in his hands, and then the enemy was no more. Another emerged from around a corner, and FN-2187 fired again. There was a rhythm to it, and his shots were going where he wanted them. A new target appeared, and he tracked it, fired while moving, scored the hit. The targets started coming faster, and he thought maybe that would take his mind off what had happened, but instead it was just the opposite and he couldn't stop thinking about the miners.

He couldn't stop thinking about how Phasma had spoken to his fire-team even as the negotiators' bodies were cooling on the floor. How she'd moved to stand directly in front of Slip.

"I was concerned about you, FN-2003," she said. "I am glad you've proven me wrong."

"Thank you, Captain."

"You're now stormtroopers," she said. Her

helmet had turned, moving from Slip to Zeroes to Nines, then finally to FN-2187. It seemed she'd held her gaze on him longer than the others. Then she'd addressed them all, tapping her breastplate to emphasize her words. "You're now one of us."

Zeroes and Nines and especially Slip, they'd felt it, they *believed* her. All the way back up to the docking bay, into the shuttle, on the flight back to the Star Destroyer, they had been barely able to contain themselves, their excitement, their relief, their pride. Even the veterans had sensed it, had invited them to share a meal in the galley to celebrate.

FN-2187 had begged off. He had training to do, he said. He needed to put in some range time.

And because they'd already labeled him an outsider, nobody argued with him and asked him to come along. Not even Slip.

The problem had to be with him, FN-2187 thought. That was the only explanation. It was what everyone had been saying all along, after all. He was different. Maybe he was so different he was broken. So he would work to fix it, to be a real stormtrooper, to be one of them. That was, he thought, what he wanted most of all. Not to be alone.

So he worked through the simulation, and it grew harder and harder, and still his shots were unerring. It wasn't until the civilians began to enter the scenario that he ran into trouble. At first they appeared only as random bystanders, obstacles to be avoided. Then there were more of them, and more, and more. Men and women and children, and suddenly FN-2187 could see only them and not the enemy hiding among them. He could see only those innocents, and in that moment he could no longer pull the trigger.

In that moment he understood it had never been a game.

He understood that he was never going to be one of them.

Captain Phasma watched FN-2187 on the monitor in her quarters. He'd stopped firing, stopped even moving, and was just standing amid the ever-changing field of moving figures.

She sighed. She'd had such hope for FN-2187. He had shown such remarkable promise. He had shown the capacity to be special.

She picked up the orders on her desk and

reviewed them once more. They'd already made the jump to hyperspace, and she knew it would be less than an hour before they reached their rendezvous point to take on their new passenger. Kylo Ren had already transmitted the coordinates for where they would be headed next.

On the monitor, FN-2187 had turned away from the still-running simulation. Harmless blaster bolts from Republic enemies peppered his back, hit after hit. Over the speakers, she could hear the computer in the simulation room declaring the scenario a failure. FN-2187 didn't seem to notice, didn't seem to care. She watched as the holographic images faded, as the room emptied to one lone stormtrooper, and then as FN-2187 walked out.

She switched off the monitor. He'd be part of the detail when they reached the landing point on Jakku, she decided. Perhaps when someone was shooting back at him, he would understand what it meant to be a real stormtrooper, what it meant to serve the First Order, body and soul.

She would give him one more chance, Phasma decided.

One last chance for FN-2187 to decide his fate.

REY

THE TEEDOS called the storm *X'us'R'iia*. It
had a name because the Teedos believed
there was only the one, the same one that
returned again and again. It was the breath of
the god R'iia, the Teedos said.

R'iia was not a benevolent god, and thus the
storm was blamed for a great many things. It
was the source of the famine that had plagued
that part of Jakku for years. It was the reason
the water had gone away. It was why their luggabeasts turned unruly. It was responsible for the
interlopers who plagued their lands. It was, sig-
nificantly, what had brought the great shards of
metal filled with many, many soft beings crashing to the sands so many years before. The ship

graveyards were a monument to R'iia's anger, the Teedos said. They were a warning, one that the interlopers in Niima consistently failed to heed, much to the Teedos' annoyance. Most of the Teedos were harmless, scavengers in their own way, much like Rey and the others. There were orthodox Teedos, though, zealots who were known to attack both their brethren and the salvagers, claiming what they did was a blasphemy to R'iia. R'iia would punish them all for their sins. The *X'us'R'iia* would punish them all.

Rey didn't believe a word of it, but she didn't believe in much outside of herself.

She'd been high on the superstructure of one of the old battle cruisers half-buried in the sands, hoping to find something to salvage that the other scavengers had missed. She looked out and saw the storm forming on the horizon. She knew immediately that it would be a big one. It was time to go.

She'd been free-climbing the wreck, and it was—perhaps paradoxically—always quicker going up than it was going down. Going down, you had to worry about gravity in a whole different way, and hurrying was a good plan to get yourself hurt.

She knew that from experience. She took it fast, anyway—almost too fast—then risked jumping the last three meters to the ground. The sand could be soft if you were close enough, but she wasn't. From that height, it was like landing on metal. The shock of impact jarred her ankles and ran a sharp pain up her calves and into her knees. She used her staff to right herself and sprinted for her speeder.

Then it was a race for home, Rey and the speeder shooting as fast as she could push it across the desert, the rising wind chasing her. With one hand she tugged the end of her long, looped scarf from beneath her belt and wrapped it around her nose and mouth. Not for the first time, she wished she owned a pair of goggles, cursed herself for not having jury-rigged some months before. The last pair she'd found, she'd traded to Unkar in Niima for two portions, barely enough food to silence her stomach for a day. It had been a bad trade when she made it, and she'd known it. She'd been hungry, told herself she'd find another pair soon enough, made the trade anyway.

That had been almost three months before.

The storm had almost caught her by the time she reached the wreckage of the walker. It came in surges, strong enough to buffet the speeder from behind, and Rey had to fight to keep the vehicle steady on its repulsors. Sand was swirling when she slid to a stop and dismounted. She shoved the speeder between two of the broken, bent legs of the giant machine and into the shelter. The sound of the storm was growing deafening, the wind a near-constant shriek, mixed with the rasping, cruel noise of sand scraping the hull of the walker. Thunder exploded above Rey, making her flinch, and she squinted skyward in time to see the last of the sunlight being eaten away by the swirling dust clouds. Dry lightning arced and lit the sky as if daylight had returned at once, just for a second. When she closed her eyes, she could still see the lightning flash. Her skin stung with biting sand, the wind trying to take her by the feet and lift her, and she had to fight her way to the side of the hull using handholds. She barely managed to wrench the makeshift door open enough to stumble inside, and then, just as quickly, slammed it shut again.

For a moment, Rey stood in the darkness of

her home, catching her breath, listening to R'iia's rage outside. The noise was diminished but still sunk through the walker's armored hull. She reached out, fumbled for a second, then found one of her lamps and triggered the key. The light flickered weakly at first, then stabilized into a warmer glow.

Rey sighed, took off her boots, and emptied sand from them. She shook off her clothes. She shook out her hair. When she was finished, there was a substantial pile of Jakku's desert at her feet, and she felt easily ten kilos lighter.

Thunder detonated overhead again, vibrating through the metal shell of the walker. Bits and pieces of various salvage jumped. One of the old helmets fell from where it hung on a makeshift hook. She lived in what had once been the main troop compartment of the walking tank, but that had been when the thing was upright. The interior had long before been stripped of anything salvageable and now resembled a cluttered workshop more than anything else. Rey had traded for a generator a couple of years before, so she had power when she needed it, mostly for the workbench where she would take apart and reassemble and, more often than not, rebuild from scratch those pieces of usable junk she recovered.

Unkar always paid more for things that still worked.

Through a hairline crack in the hull, Rey saw a sudden flare of light, more dry lightning. She picked up one of the blankets on the floor and used it to cover the crack. She secured it using three of the rare magnets she'd recovered from a shattered gyro-stabilizer. She went to her stash, hidden beneath one of the side panels, unscrewed the plate, and removed one of the three bottles of water she'd left there. She took a drink to wash the desert out of her mouth, swallowed with a grimace, carefully recapped the bottle, and just as carefully restored it to its hiding place before securing the panel.

She sat on the pile of remaining blankets and rested her head against the back of the hull, listening to the storm beat furiously against her home.

She closed her eyes, feeling, for the first time in a very long time, very much alone.

The *X'us'R'iia* lasted three and a half days.

Rey finished one bottle of water and half of

another, guarding her thirst, because she didn't know how long it would be until she'd be able to get into Niima for more. She was out of food by the second day, and by the time the storm was over her headache was so intense she was light-headed and had to go slowly when she moved around her little home.

She'd jury-rigged a computer using pieces scavenged from several crashed fighters over the years, including a cracked but still-usable display from an old BTL-A4 Y-wing. There were no radio communications to speak of—no way to transmit or receive and, frankly, nobody she wanted to talk to anyway. On the wreckage of a Zephra-series hauler, though, she'd once found a stash of data chips, and after painstakingly going through each and every one of them, she'd discovered three with their programs intact; one of them, to her delight, had been a flight simulator.

So when she wasn't sleeping or just sitting and listening to the storm or tinkering at her work-bench, she flew. It was a good program, or at least she imagined it was. She could select any number of ships to fly, from small repulsor-driven atmospheric craft to a wide variety of fighters, all the way up to an array of stock freighters. She could set destinations, worlds she'd never visited and never imagined she would, and scenarios, from speed runs to obstacle courses to system failures.

At first, she'd been truly horrible at it, quite literally crashing a few seconds after takeoff every time. With nothing else to do, and with a perverse sense of determination that she would *not* allow herself to be beaten by a machine that she herself had put together with her own hands, she learned. She learned so much that there was little the program could throw her way that would challenge her now. She'd gotten to the point where she would, quite deliberately, do everything she could think of to make things hard on herself, just to see if she could get out of it. Full-throttle atmospheric reentry with repulsor-engine failure? No sweat. Multiple hull breach deep-space engine flameout? A walk in the park.

It was, if nothing else, a way to pass the time.

When Rey finally ventured out, it took her an hour to get her door open. The sand was piled so high and packed so hard against it that she could move it only by centimeters at first. With each push, more of the desert rushed into her home.

When she finally *did* have the door open, she had to spend another hour cleaning up, but that was mostly because she was working very slowly. Every time she bent and straightened up again, the lightheadedness would return and she would have to stop and steady herself with a hand on the wall.

The sun was hot and mean when she finally emerged. Miraculously, her speeder had been spared the worst of the storm. She dusted it off, checked the power, started the engine, and was pleasantly surprised when it responded without hesitation. She went back inside long enough to get her staff and a few pieces from her workbench to offer Unkar. She then closed up, mounted her speeder, and took the drive into Niima. She went slowly, mindful that she wasn't at her best.

The little town—if you could call it a town, and she wasn't certain you could, but she didn't have much to compare it with—was still nearly deserted. The tarps over the washing station had been shredded by the *X'us'R'iia*, and there were two sentries out working on repairs. Rey parked between the station and Unkar's place and looked over at the little airfield out of habit, counting the ships. There were the same three ships parked there, the same three as ever. All of them looked like they'd survived the storm without damage.

She trudged over to Unkar's window, feeling the sun pummeling her. He was already there, watching with swollen eyes in a bloated face.

"First one in," he said.

Rey dug in her satchel, pulled out the three pieces of salvage she'd taken from her bench, and set them on the counter between them. "What'll you give me?"

One of Unkar's thick hands reached out, palming the pieces one at a time and pulling them through the opening so he could examine them more closely. Rey waited, glancing about. More people were arriving, venturing out after the storm. A couple of other salvagers apparently had gone out hunting first and were making their way to the washing station to clean up their finds. Rey cursed herself quietly for not having done the same. The storm would've shifted the sands in the graveyard. Who knew what it might've uncovered? By the time she got out there, there'd be nothing left.

"What's this supposed to be?" Unkar asked.

Rey looked at the piece in his hand. "It's the actuator for a Kuat-7 acceleration compensator."

"Not like this it isn't. And this, this supposed to be part of a data buffer set?"

"Yeah."

Unkar grunted. "This one is good, low-interference regulator for a Z-70, I can move this." He spread the three pieces out between them. "Give you three portions, one for each of them."

"The Z-70 is worth three alone, Unkar."

"I'm offering you three, Rey. Take it or leave it."

She winced. The sunlight was making her headache worse.

"Three portions, two bottles of water," Rey said.

She was eating the muck that passed for a meal—one portion—in the shade by the vendor stalls when she heard the engines. Everyone looked up, Rey included. They all watched as the ship came in lazily over the airfield, then set down with a whisper. It was an old *Hernon*-class light freighter, boxy and ugly. Rey had seen it there maybe ten times before, and so had everyone else; just as quickly their attention strayed from the arrival back to the various tasks at hand. Unkar did a lot of repeat business with some traders, people looking to buy his salvage on the cheap and off the books.

There were a few dregs of the blue slop remaining in the packet in her hand, and Rey brought it to her lips and squeezed what was left into her mouth. She got up and wandered toward the washing station, now with every position filled and another half dozen fellow salvagers waiting their turns. She tossed the package in the trash and looked back at the airfield. The ramp had dropped, and the first figure to emerge was exactly the one she'd expected: the same human she'd seen there every other time. He stopped at the bottom of the ramp and turned back to speak to someone still aboard, and Rey saw another figure descending, a young girl, followed by yet a third, an older woman. Those were new faces to her, and Rey found herself staring.

The man gestured toward Unkar's, speaking to the woman and the girl. The girl stuck her hands in her pockets, shoulders dropping, and the woman put her hand on the girl's head as she spoke to the man. The man lowered his hands and set them both on the girl's shoulders. She looked up at him and he bent toward her, maybe speaking, and then pointed into the ship. The girl turned and followed the woman back up the ramp and out of sight. The man headed for Unkar's.

Rey returned to her speeder, trying to imagine what the exchange had been about—what the girl had said, what the man had said, what the woman had said. She kicked the engine to life and wheeled her speeder back toward the desert, mulling that over.

She didn't have the first idea what it had all been about.

Rey didn't have much hope for a good find. She'd lost the morning already, and by the time she'd ridden her speeder out to the edges of the graveyard, it was midafternoon. Anything the storm had revealed farther in had already been claimed. As she rode, she could see small groups of scavengers working new wrecks. A lot of people worked in teams, figuring they could cover more ground that way. Rey worked alone and always had. It was easier when she was alone; there were fewer complications, fewer things to worry about. The only person she had to trust was herself.

She rode out farther, beyond the easy finds and into the harder terrain. She was feeling better, the meal having satisfied the gnawing hunger, at least for the moment, and she opened up the speeder. Rey rode fast and hard, enjoying the thrill of the machine's power and acceleration. She'd had the speeder for years, built it herself as she had so many other things, and as much as she could allow herself a sense of pride in anything, she was proud of that.

The graveyard wasn't, strictly speaking, just *one* area but a vast expanse, and you could go for kilometers without seeing signs of anything, then crest some high dune and suddenly find yourself looking down at a field of wreckage. The storm had done more than reveal new finds, however; it had changed the terrain, reshaped the desert, and it wasn't until she hit the Crackle and saw the Spike that Rey realized how far out she'd gone, how long she'd been riding. The Crackle was one of the few constants in the desert, marked by the almost perfectly vertical spine of some massive capital ship—the Spike—half-buried in the ground. Nobody knew what kind of ship it had been, Republic, Imperial, something else from earlier; it was impossible to tell, because all that remained was the keel line, rising out of the ground, and some twisted support beams still clinging to what remained of the frame. Everything else of the ship was simply gone, taken in the explosion of plasma that had erupted on impact. The heat had been so intense it had seared the desert sand, burning so fast and hot it had turned the ground to blackened glass. Over the years, the glass had broken into smaller and smaller chunks, on its way to becoming sand once more, but when you rode or walked over the land, you'd hear it cracking, echoes that seemed to whisper for kilometers.

Hence the Crackle.

Rey stopped as she approached the Spike, squinting up at the sun as she pulled a corner of her wrap from her face. Maybe two hours of daylight left, she calculated, and she'd need most of that to get back home. The temperature plummeted at night, got as cold as it could be hot during the day. What little wildlife there was on that part of Jakku emerged in the darkness, as well, and most of it was predatory, as desperate to survive as every other living thing. The swarms of gnaw-jaws came out at night, carnivores that ran on six legs and preyed on warm blood. Getting caught in the dark wouldn't be good.

She'd lost the day, Rey concluded, but maybe she could get a head start on the next one. She shut down the speeder, dismounted, and spat out more sand. She drank half of one of the bottles she'd gotten from Unkar, then stowed it back in her satchel. Rey looked at the Spike critically, thinking. It was definitely climbable. Not particularly safe but climbable.

Slipping the staff from her back, Rey left it leaning against the side of the speeder and made her way to the base of the Spike. The ground broke beneath her boots, glass popping and cracking. The pillar creaked as she reached its base, the Spike resettling in the sand, as if warning Rey to reconsider her plan.

The metal, hot from a day in the sun, burned under her hands as she climbed. She used the edges of her wrap as makeshift gloves, but still the heat seeped through. There were more hand-holds and footholds than it had at first seemed, and she ascended quickly, focusing on what she was doing rather than what was above or quickly growing farther away below. It wasn't until she felt the wind snapping the ends of her scarf that she realized how high she'd gone. Rey stopped, then wedged herself into a gap on the Spike where she could almost sit. It wasn't comfortable, but it was secure, at least for the moment.

The view was amazing. She'd climbed easily one hundred meters, maybe higher, she thought. Looking back the direction she'd come, she could just make out what she guessed was Niima, shimmering and distorted in the heat haze. Between her and the town stretched the majority of the known graveyard, the edge marked by the dead Star Destroyer, and from there even that appeared small. Rey shifted her weight to the side and pulled her macrobinoculars from her satchel. Only one of the lenses worked, so it was more a macromonocular, she figured, but it worked all the same. She brought it to her eyes and scanned the desert spread out before her.

There were a couple of Teedos on the horizon,

the range finder on the macros telling her they were over fifty kilometers out. They were walking their luggabeasts instead of riding them, which meant they'd been out on a long search and were returning home. She swept her gaze to the left, over the featureless desert. It was disappointing. There was nothing new to see, and the few wrecks she knew to be out that way were gone now, eaten once more by the desert.

Something dug at her vision, a flash—metal or glass—just for an instant, and Rey swung her view back, slower, and felt her heartbeat quickening. She forced herself to look slowly and tried to retrace the path her eyes had taken, but it took genuine willpower to do it. The sun was dropping, and Rey knew that whatever the light had caught, it had been a case of right place, right time; in minutes, perhaps even seconds, the sun would drop even lower, and what had been revealed might vanish forever.

She saw it again—the flare of sunlight glinting off exposed metal—and she refocused the macros and pulled out. What she found nearly made Rey fall off the Spike.

It was a ship.

Rey lowered the macros. She checked the sun again. By the time she climbed down, she'd have just enough time to make it back home before darkness fell. If she pushed to the wreck she would make it with daylight left, but there'd be no way to get back to the walker before the desert turned cold and dangerous with nightfall and everything that came with it. She could leave it for tomorrow, head out at dawn, and hope that she would be able to find the wreck again and that nobody else would discover it before she could claim it.

It was those last two unknowns that made her decision: the fear that she would never be able to find it again and that someone would steal it from her.

She stuffed the macros back in her satchel and began the long climb down.

It was an old Ghtroc Industries 690, a small light freighter, and Rey recognized it instantly from her flight sim; she'd flown and crashed the later version, the 720, more times than she could count. The sun was kissing the horizon, bathing everything in soft gold light, and it made the ship look every bit as precious as Rey knew it was, because the greatest miracle of all—more than the fact that it hadn't yet been discovered and claimed by anyone, as far as she could tell, more than the fact that it was almost entirely uncovered—was that the ship was *intact*.

There was absolutely damage. She could see that even as she hopped off her speeder and stood staring at the vessel. The telemetry dish had been sheared from the top of the hull, and the cockpit windshield was missing several panes, presumably shattered on impact, and the two that remained were webbed with cracks. Along the hull to her left—the starboard side, Rey told herself—there was a gash that ran almost two meters and exposed corroded, melted wiring and hunks of missing cable. Whoever had brought it down had tried to take it through its landing cycle, and the front landing strut, at least as best she could see where the sand had shifted, was missing entirely.

But it was a ship, it was in one piece, and Rey had found it—and that made it hers. Her face felt strange; she had an odd ache in her cheeks, and as she went closer, she caught her reflection in what was left of the cockpit's windshield. She was filthy, but that was normal. What surprised her was that she was smiling, and when she tried to stop, the ache in her cheeks remained and she found that she was still doing it anyway.

Unkar would pay . . . Rey tried to calculate what Unkar would pay for the ship, just like that. A hundred portions? Five hundred? Enough food that she could eat for a year. With water and maybe some other things, too: better tools, perhaps, or even a blaster so she could better protect herself, instead of having to rely on her staff. All that just for the wreck, and that didn't even count anything Rey might find inside.

Shadows were starting to stretch from the freighter across the sand. She was losing the light. Quickly, she pushed her speeder into cover beneath the cockpit, which was jutting up at a twenty-degree angle. She switched off the power, then scrambled around the side of the dune, trying to get a better look at the ship. It had listed to port, either because of the storm or simply the way it had gone down, and a large dune was beginning to sweep over the hull on that side. Another day, a strong wind, and the whole ship might end up hidden again.

Sand slid beneath her feet as she summited

the dune. With a running start, Rey leapt down and landed atop the hull. The exterior of the ship was burning hot, still holding the heat of the day, and she hissed in pain as she pushed herself back to her feet. She could feel the burn through her boots. The ship remained stable. It didn't rock or wobble as she worked her way forward toward the cockpit. One of the missing panes was wide enough for her to slip through. Looking down she saw where the desert had spilled into the freighter, making almost a ramp of sand to aid her descent. She got down on her hands and knees, gritted her teeth when the hot metal burned her, and crawled inside. Once she was through she rolled onto her back and slid the rest of the way down.

Rey ended up between two seats, the pilot and copilot positions. It was much cooler inside and strangely silent. The noise of the desert, which seemed quiet at the best of times, was entirely gone. There was nothing, just stillness. Ahead of her, the cockpit door hung half-open, its panels split and akimbo, and beyond that there was only darkness.

Rey slid in the sand as she got to her feet and

put a hand on the back of the pilot's chair to steady herself. Something fell from the headrest and clattered against metal. Her eyes were still adjusting to the dimness, and it took a moment before she recognized what she'd knocked free. She found herself smiling again, despite herself.

She picked up the fallen goggles and blew sand clear of the lenses. She held them up, examining them. There wasn't a scratch on them. Rey slung the goggles around her neck, then pulled her flashlight from her satchel.

She set out to explore her find.

Rey's biggest fear was that she would find a body or, worse, bodies, whatever remained of the unfortunate crew. She figured someone had to have taken the ship down, a pilot who'd started the landing cycle all those years before. It was quite conceivable it had been the last thing the pilot had ever done. So she was cautious, not because she was squeamish but because she didn't want to be surprised by a corpse.

There was no body to find, and there was a logical explanation for that: the freighter was missing both its escape pods. The landing cycle,

Rey guessed, had been initiated by the autopilot in an attempt to save the ship.

The Ghtroc was a small ship, especially for a freighter. The 720, the model she was more familiar with, had been designed for a maximum crew of two, with room for another eight passengers and 135 metric tons of cargo capacity. The 690 was scaled down from that in all ways, designed for a crew of one, with room for three passengers and only 60 metric tons of cargo capacity.

She made her way with care, working from the cockpit back. Due to the way the ship had settled, moving through it was treacherous though not unmanageable. Rey had to go slowly because she needed one hand to steady herself, the other for her light. She found the crew quarters, along with evidence of two people—old clothes and personal belongings—which she left alone. She found the galley and saw that half the rations had spoiled or gone to dust, but there were seventeen quick-meal packs still intact and sealed and a purifier jug that would turn dirty water into something she could drink. She almost laughed with joy.

When Rey saw the green light, though, she *did* laugh.

The reactor core was to the aft, and it should've been dead. There should've been no power running to any system aboard. She almost missed it. She thought it was a reflection from her flashlight, an afterimage, but when she turned away it clung to her peripheral vision. She half-slid to the main control panel. She was so excited she couldn't catch her breath. The light was weak, but it was there, it was real, and it illuminated two words on the button. Her heart in her throat, Rey pressed it.

Overhead and all around her, lights flickered to life as auxiliary power was restored to the freighter.

If Unkar would pay five hundred portions for the wreck . . . what would he pay for a wreck that wasn't a wreck? What would he pay for a *ship*?

And the craziest idea of all, the one she'd been trying to ignore since she'd slid into the cockpit, the one she hadn't allowed herself to entertain because it was dangerously close to hope: what would Unkar pay for a ship that *worked*?

Rey spent the night on the freighter. She shut down the auxiliary power, both to prevent the batteries from draining any further and to keep light from leaking out of the ship. Her greatest fear was discovery, what would happen if someone else found her ship. They would undoubtedly try to take it from her; they would try to steal what was now hers. She wasn't going to let that happen.

She tried one of the beds in the crew cabin for sleep but found two things wrong with that plan. The first was that the angle of the ship meant she slid against the bulkhead with all her weight on her side. That was uncomfortable but bearable. The second, however, was the bed itself. It was far too soft. She ended up on the floor.

First thing in the morning, Rey broke the seal on one of the quick-meals and ate, what was to her, some of the finest food she'd ever enjoyed. She had no idea what it was, but there was actual meat product and a sauce that was sweet and tangy at the same time and something she thought might be nuts, which popped between her teeth with a satisfying snap. There was also a small disk, encased in some sort of batter, and when she bit into that it mixed with an almost spicy sugar that was so intense she nearly gagged on its sweetness.

The next order of business was protecting the ship from prying eyes. That was apparently something the previous owners had wanted, as well, because as Rey searched the cargo hold for something to cover the freighter, she found a displaced floor panel and, after some muscle and prying, managed to pop it open to reveal two folded sheets. Unfolding one, she discovered it was much larger than she'd first thought. There was an actuator tab on one corner, and Rey pressed it, not knowing what to expect. Still holding the edge of the enormous blanket, she watched it literally disappear before her eyes or, more precisely, blend to match its surroundings. When she pressed the actuator again, the fabric reverted to a dull flat gray. She remembered a Klatooinian salvager arguing with Unkar about something like that but much smaller. A memetic sheet, he'd called it.

Rey concluded that whoever had owned the freighter before her hadn't, perhaps, been concerned with operating legally.

It took a while and some scrambling around the hull to get the two sheets positioned over her freighter and weighted down so they wouldn't get away in a sudden gust of wind. Once activated, the ship all but vanished into the surrounding terrain. Rey didn't have any idea how long the sheets would last, if they needed recharging or worked on a battery or even solar power—solar power would've been very nice, she thought—but they did the job well enough. You would have to be almost on top of the freighter before you realized there was something there besides desert.

Rey climbed back inside. She was growing more familiar with the ship and was having an easier time moving about. She'd found an old paper notebook in the crew quarters and a couple of styluses for writing, and she took them with her when she switched the auxiliary power back on and brought the lights up once more. Then she set to work making a very careful inventory of the ship's systems, working from the engines forward to the cockpit. She checked wiring, power couplings, cabling, conduits, rigging, component plating, circuitry. She was methodical and patient, and she filled page after page of the notebook with her findings: what worked, what didn't, what needed repair, what could be jury-rigged, what would need to be salvaged from other vessels, what would have to be traded for or, worse, bought.

It took four days for Rey to complete the list, and when she finished she treated herself to another of the quick-meals—she was down to eleven of them, and those battered disks were definitely her favorite. She looked over everything she'd written and wondered if it would be worth it to continue. It was an enormous amount of work. Most of the things on her list she could repair or jury-rig herself, but some of the items would need to be replaced entirely or rebuilt from scratch. Things like the missing cockpit windshield panes could be hunted down, but it would take time. Corroded wiring and missing couplings and conduits could be picked off of other pieces of salvage. But the premix chamber for the hyperdrive engines needed a new containment unit, and Rey didn't have either the know-how or the facilities to make one herself. The portside dorsal repulsorlift emitter was totaled, and while it wasn't strictly needed to fly—there were three other emitters and they all seemed relatively intact—not having it would make takeoff and landing a challenge. Never mind the fact that, perhaps most crucial of all, the ship had no fuel left, only what remained in the auxiliary batteries.

Without fuel, there was no way she'd be able to fly her little freighter into Niima.

That was something, Rey realized, she actually *wanted*. She wanted to be the ship that everyone looked up and stared at. She wanted to see the expressions on everyone's faces as she came down the ramp and they saw it was her, Rey, who had flown that prize home. She wanted to see Unkar's big eyes open wide and his face puff up in surprise, to hear him stammer as he made offer after offer for the ship, *her* ship, before she agreed.

Five hundred portions? Try five *thousand* portions, Unkar. Try five thousand portions and a new speeder, a new set of tools, a spare generator, and the first pick of salvage that comes in for, say, the next two—no, four, no, *five*—years.

She wanted that very much.

That meant, she realized, it was time to get to work.

The task was even harder and slower than Rey had imagined. Problems magnified and grew exponentially, and it wasn't simply with the repairs to her ship. That would have been bad enough, just trying to get everything aboard working again.

That would've been a full-time job in and of itself.

She still needed to eat. She still needed to survive. She still needed to work, and that meant she had to work twice as hard, because she was effectively trying to gather salvage for two jobs. Every piece of salvage she managed to collect was now subjected to critical evaluation: was it for the ship or for Unkar? The best pieces, of course, were worth the most to Unkar and could bring multiple portions. Invariably, those same pieces were the ones Rey needed to repair her ship. The harder it was to replace, the more it was worth; the harder it was to replace, the less likely that Rey would find another.

For that reason, the ship *had* to come first; it had to be the priority. If it wasn't, then all that work was for nothing. Two months, then three, then five passed, and she was almost always hungry, sometimes going two days without a meal before finally, begrudgingly trading Unkar for more than just one portion at a time. Days spent crawling through the graveyard, desperately searching for bits and pieces, racking her brain trying to remember where she had seen an oscillation gyro that might still work, an intact plate of duralloy shielding that was big enough to help seal the gash in her freighter's side, a coercive reciprocating pump for the oxygen scrubbers. It was exhausting. It was unending.

It took its toll, and Rey wasn't as careful as she might have been.

Much of what she salvaged, whether to be used on her freighter or traded to Unkar, needed to be cleaned. Rey would use the washing station at Niima, picking the times when the fewest people were around. She would scrub the filth and dirt and sand from her pieces, set them aside to dry, and then, as surreptitiously as she could, slip those components she needed for repairs back into her satchel. Some things she took in had no obvious salvage value at all but still needed to be washed. Cabling, for instance, was relatively easy to find but less than worthless as far as Unkar was concerned.

"What're you building?"

Rey was bent down, scrubbing a particularly stubborn chunk of carbon scoring from a band limiter. She lifted her head sharply and stared the questioner accusingly in the eyes. The speaker was a human female, shorter than Rey but about her age. Her hair was short, shaved on the sides. Rey tried to remember her name.

"Devi."

"Yeah," the woman said. "You're Rey, right? What're you building?"

"I'm not building anything."

"Unkar's not gonna pay for that. Porto's crew brought in, like, maybe a hundred band limiters in the last week. You gotta know that."

Rey shook the component dry and shoved it into her satchel, hoping the conversation was over.

It wasn't. Devi looked to her side, and her partner—another human, almost a head taller than Rey, with his hair shorn identically to Devi's—slid onto the stool beside Rey. Devi took the one opposite.

"You know Strunk, right?" Devi asked.

Rey began gathering the pieces she'd set out to dry. Her staff was to her left, in easy reach, opposite where Strunk had taken a seat. Rey wondered if she would have to use it.

"You hold pieces back." Devi scratched her

chin, leaving a smear of grease behind. "We've seen it. Like, you had the junction box for a power inverter on the YT series a couple days ago. That could've gotten you a lot. But you didn't trade it."

"Doing a lot with circuits and cabling, too," Strunk said. "Like you're wiring something up, you know?"

Rey stared at him. Strunk shrugged and smiled apologetically.

"We don't mean to pry, Rey," Devi said. "We're just curious, is all. You've not been around as much as you used to, and it's just . . . you know, it's just strange. Like, why would you not trade that stuff, you know?"

"I'm not that hungry," Rey said.

Devi looked surprised. Then she laughed. "Sure, okay. I get it. We all mind our own business. I get it."

"Yes," Rey said. "That's what we do."

Strunk nodded. Rey stuffed the remaining components into her satchel, grabbed her staff, and got to her feet.

"Nice talking to you," Rey said.

"Hey."

Rey turned back to Devi.

"Thing is," Devi said, "we've noticed. So maybe somebody else has, like, noticed, too. Know what I mean?"

Devi tilted her head ever so slightly in the direction of Unkar's window. Rey couldn't see him there, but that didn't mean he wasn't watching. She looked back at Devi.

"I'll keep it in mind," Rey said.

It was another ten days before they found her. Rey knew it was coming. The two memetic sheets that had kept the freighter hidden had died, one after the other, the same day she'd spoken to them in Niima, and as a result she had to resort to throwing shovelfuls of sand over the hull of the ship. It was a weak concealment, and every time the wind picked up the hull would be revealed for anyone close enough to see.

She tried to be more careful, but there were just too many places to hide amid the graveyard, too many places to keep watch. If Devi and Strunk were really on to her, all they needed to be was patient and eventually they'd see Rey on her speeder, heading out. They would follow, and it wouldn't matter how many times Rey switched directions or doubled back, if she rode out in the morning or the afternoon. She would be seen. So it was never really a question of *if* but *when*, and Rey accepted that.

She was on her back in the crawl space off the cockpit, trying to get the navicomputer relays reconnected, when she heard them outside.

"Rey?" It was Devi. "Hey, Rey, you in there?"

Rey sighed, then pulled herself up and out of the floor. She set the microblade beside the rest of her tools, grabbed her staff, and headed into the cockpit. Devi and Strunk were both standing outside. Devi was grinning and Strunk's mouth was open, as if he couldn't believe what he was seeing.

"What?" Rey asked, then added, "Do you want?"

"This is *amazing!*" Strunk shouted, as if snapping out of a trance. "R'iia's shorts, Rey! This is *amazing!*"

"It's just a ship," Rey said.

Devi laughed. "Just a ship? You're crazy! Look at this thing! How'd you find it?"

Rey climbed into the pilot's seat, pulled herself out of the half-repaired cockpit, and dropped onto the sand. She held her staff in both hands, leaning on it, but it would be easy enough to move it into a swing if necessary. She looked first at Strunk, then at Devi.

"I figured it had to be something," Devi said. "I knew you were working on *something* big, but, like, no way I ever imagined it was something like this. I thought maybe one of the ground vehicles or a repulsortank or something like that. Never imagined this! Rey, you've got a ship, girl! You've found yourself a ship!"

"It needs a lot of work." Rey's voice sounded odd to her ears, as if she were speaking just to say something, but there was pride in it, too.

"Yeah, I'll bet." Devi stepped forward, craning her head back to look at the exposed underbelly. "Looks like one of the repulsors is totaled. And the landing gear."

"There's a Ghtroc 720," Strunk said. He spoke slowly. "You know the one? Out by Feressee's Point? The one that split when it came down? It's all upside down and in pieces, but it's still got its gear. This is a Ghtroc, right?"

"The 690," Rey said.

"Two of us could move it," Devi said, excited.

"Be about a day's work, maybe two, get it cut free and haul it back over here."

They were both looking at her.

"It's my ship," Rey said after a long pause.

"We can help you," Devi said. "C'mon. Strunk's big and strong and stupid, so he's fearless, like, and I'm small and smart and can get into the tiny crawl spaces. We can help you fix this thing up, Rey."

"And what do you get out of it?"

"You take us with you," Devi said.

Rey blinked. The sentence didn't make sense to her, not at all. "Where?"

"Wherever it is you're going."

"I'm going to Niima. I'm going to sell it to Unkar."

Strunk opened his mouth to speak, but Devi moved her hand in a way that Rey understood was meant to shut him up. Strunk closed his mouth and shrugged.

"Unkar'll pay a lot for it, especially if it's spaceworthy," Devi said. She nodded, agreeing with herself. "Yeah, figure, what? Six, maybe seven thousand portions? He'd go higher if it'll do hyperspace."

"The converter chamber fractured," Rey said. "If I can find a replacement and fit it, it can do hyperspace. It needs fuel."

Devi nodded, enthusiastic. "Sure, yeah, perfect! We help you fix it up, we do shares of the sale, split whatever Unkar's willing to pay. That's what I'm thinking. That's fair, right? Each of us gets, like, a third?"

"It's my ship."

"Right, that's fair, too, your ship, you found it. So you get half, and Strunk and I split the rest. That's gonna be five thousand shares for you, at least. Unkar'll fall all over himself for this, you know he will."

Rey didn't say anything, thinking. The split didn't seem fair to her somehow, but she wasn't entirely certain what fair was.

Devi looked up at the hull again, as if admiring the ship. "In fact, he'd probably fall all over himself for this just as it is, right now."

Strunk had his hands in his pockets and was looking down, but he glanced at Devi for a moment before returning his eyes to his boots. Devi was turning slowly in place, still taking in the lines of the hull.

It wasn't an overt threat, Rey knew. The way Devi had said it, maybe it hadn't been meant as a threat at all but rather an observation, a statement of fact about Unkar's greed and the worth of Rey's little light freighter. The problem was, of course, that there was no way to be sure. There was no way to be certain that, if Rey refused their help, they'd forget about the ship and leave her alone. No way to be certain that they wouldn't go to Unkar and tell him about the ship and claim the finder's fee on it, if nothing else. The more Rey thought about that, the more she realized she couldn't trust them not to do it. If she couldn't trust them to keep it secret, how could she trust them to help her repair it?

But there didn't seem any other option.

"What do you say?" Devi asked. She was looking at Rey again. "Partners?"

Rey looked at her hands, where they met on her staff. Her fingers were filthy, her nails cracked and grease stained. She considered her options and didn't like any of them. She sighed.

"Let me show you around," Rey said.

The benefits of working with Devi and Strunk were immediate, much to Rey's initial annoyance.

She was so used to being alone that having them around the ship—*her* ship—set her teeth on edge. And Devi talked all the time, which made it worse.

But they were good salvagers, and there was no denying that fact. They knew the graveyard as well as Rey did, but like everyone working in the deserts of Jakku, they had discovered their own prime spots, their own special finds that they'd kept hidden from everyone else. Many of the parts that Rey had begun to despair of ever repairing, let alone replacing, Devi and Strunk were able to produce in a matter of days. They brought in the promised landing strut within the first twenty-four hours; three days later, they showed up in the afternoon dragging an entire repulsorlift complex that they'd pulled, whole, from a crashed *Lambda*-class shuttle. It was an Imperial design, never intended to incorporate with the Ghtroc's systems, but it took Rey only another day and a half to fashion an interface converter. Before the week was out, they'd replaced the missing portside generator.

Rey went up to the cockpit to check that the systems had interfaced properly. She'd replaced the batteries for the main flight system months earlier, and the ship rested in a low-power standby mode. Devi and Strunk followed her, eager and excited, watching closely as she went quickly through the power-up sequence, then initiated the repulsorlift engines. Each of the three emitters had its own gauge, blue vertical bars that measured lift power in percentages, and the fore and starboard ones responded immediately, indicating that they were fully operational.

"Did it work?" Devi asked. "Is it working?"

Rey fiddled with the port-side controller, trying to get the jury-rigged engine in synch with the other two. Its power bar remained stubbornly empty and then, all at once, jumped to full. All of them felt the ship tremble beneath them, vibrating slightly. Grains of sand bounced off the repaired canopy of the cockpit and slid down the window.

Strunk whooped, cheering inarticulately, and Devi was laughing. Devi slapped Rey on the shoulder, which annoyed Rey, but she found herself smiling anyway.

"You are amazing!" Devi said. "You are unbelievable, Rey!"

Rey squirmed in the pilot's seat. "You guys helped."

"Sure, if you call dragging chunks of starships across the desert helping! *You're* the one who put it all together. You're the one who's making this thing work!" Devi swung herself into the copilot's chair and spun it around on its post. The chair creaked as it turned. "Let's take her up!"

"What, now?"

Strunk seemed to share Rey's confusion. "Dev?"

"Sure, now," Devi said. She swept one hand toward the view out the canopy. "Sun's low enough. We stay level nobody'll see us, right? They'll be looking at the sun. Let's do it! I want to see if it'll really fly!"

Rey looked at the indicators on the console, the power levels, the temperature and pressure and flux gauges. The repulsors were idling, fully powered. The freighter was alive, trembling almost imperceptibly around them.

"You know you want to," Devi said. "You totally know you want to, Rey."

Rey put her hands on the yoke and licked her bottom lip. "Just to make sure everything's hooked up properly."

"Of course."

Rey settled her feet on the control pedals and

reached with her right to disengage the static locks. A warning light came on to tell her that the ship wasn't properly pressurized, and she switched it off, then reconfigured the controls for atmospheric flight. Devi was watching her, grinning the same as ever. Strunk had moved to stand behind Devi's seat and was holding on to the back of it so tightly Rey saw the color had gone out of his knuckles.

"First flight?" she asked him.

He nodded.

"Mine, too," Rey said.

She cut the brakes and brought up the power on the repulsors, the way she had thousands of times before in simulations. The ship moved, rising in an almost perfectly straight line, and Rey felt Jakku trying to pull her back down, her and Devi and Strunk and the ship, too, as if afraid to let them go. She felt the ship wobble slightly as she held the yoke, felt the nose dip as she came off the pedals and directed the repulsor field to propel them forward. The little freighter hesitated, as if uncertain of its relationship with gravity. Rey's stomach dropped, and Strunk made a noise that sounded like a whimper and a moan combined. Rey teased the power and fed more to the repulsors, and all at once they were sliding forward into the late afternoon sky.

They were flying.

"So amazing," Devi whispered.

Rey had to agree. According to the instruments, they were only fifty meters up and coasting at a sedate one-tenth acceleration, but the ship was alive in her hands and the world outside was changed because of it. The graveyard, the Crackle, the Spike, everything was recognizable yet entirely different seen from that new position. She could make out Niima on the horizon, the tiny specks of its huts and few buildings. She could see a lone Teedo and luggabeast traversing the desert away from the setting sun. She could see the sky changing colors, growing richer and deeper than it had ever looked from the ground.

"It works," Devi said. "It scorchin' well works, Rey!"

"It works," Rey said softly. All the repairs seemed to be holding. A few warning lights were flashing, but they were all nonessential systems, at least for the moment. The engines were still in synch and at full power.

"I'm glad it works," Strunk said. "Can we land again, please?"

Devi turned in her chair to look at him. "You big baby."

"No, he's right," Rey said. "We don't want to be seen, not yet."

"Right, yeah."

Rey banked the ship, the maneuver graceful and effortless, and circled back to where they'd lifted off. The sense of movement, the response of the freighter to her commands, had her smiling again. Her flight sim, for all its wonder and entertainment, had never captured that, and how could it? How could it have ever synthesized the reality of that freedom and power?

She set down the ship as gently as it had lifted off, powered down the engines in sequence, then put the main batteries back into standby mode. The sky had turned to dusk.

Devi got out of the copilot's seat and clapped Rey on the shoulder again. "Mechanic *and* pilot, you do it all! C'mon, Strunk, let's go home. See you tomorrow, Rey. We're gonna find that conversion chamber for the hyperdrive for you. We get that, *then* we're in business!"

Without a word, Rey watched them disembark down the boarding ramp.

———

and switched on a light long enough to find a knife. She cut a slit in the blanket's center, then pulled it over her head, wearing it as a poncho. She switched off the light, shoved the door open, and stepped into the desert night. Somewhere, out beyond the dunes, Rey heard the distant howl of a gnaw-jaw summoning its swarm.

The world was bright. The stars were magnificent and turned the desert a luminescent gray. Rey drove, goggles over her eyes and head down, the makeshift poncho weak protection against the cold. Her hands ached on the speeder's controls. She went faster than she should've but not as fast as she could, and a sickening sense of dread pushed at her from within, as if it could climb from her belly to her throat.

She wasn't afraid of violence. She didn't enjoy it, but she wasn't afraid of it. It was a necessary part of surviving on Jakku. She'd learned to defend herself early. She had been in more fights than she could remember. More wins than losses, thankfully. She was good enough that the word had spread in Niima to stay clear of her and what she could do with her staff. She could fight. She would fight, if necessary.

Devi, Rey decided, would be the dangerous

one. Strunk was strong, but he was slow and followed Devi's lead. Devi was quick, and Rey had seen the vibro-knife she carried on her belt, knew that she wore a cut-down shock stick strapped to her left leg, beneath her pants. If it came to a fight, Rey would go for Devi first. Then she'd deal with Strunk.

She wasn't looking forward to it.

The ship was exactly as Rey had left it, undisturbed and silent. She slid the speeder into cover at the aft end of the ship, then stopped and listened to the silence of the desert. There was no wind. There was no sound but her own breathing. She shivered, rubbed her aching, cold hands together, heard the sand whispering beneath her feet as she walked to the loading ramp and keyed the passcode. The ramp lowered on its hydraulics, the noise of it sudden and all the louder in the stillness of the night.

Rey climbed aboard, then shut and locked the ramp behind her. It was dark in the main compartment, lit by only the faint glow of starlight creeping in from the cockpit corridor. She followed the light into the cockpit and lowered herself into the pilot's seat. She pulled her goggles down so they hung at her neck and laid her staff across her thighs.

She felt foolish. She'd been so certain that she would arrive to find the ship already gone or, if she was lucky, Devi and Strunk in the process of trying to steal it. She had ridden through the Graveyard and across the Crackle and risked gnaw-jaws and frostbite and crashing all because she couldn't bring herself to trust them. She wondered if the situation had been reversed, if Devi and Strunk had been the ones to discover the ship and Rey had stumbled on it later, would they have felt the same? Would Rey have done to them what she was certain they planned to do to her?

She was so tired.

She shut her eyes. She felt sleep tugging at her, pulling her down. She half-dreamt of being warm, of being small, lost memories trying to swim their way to the surface. She opened her eyes, and it was still night. The stars shimmered, limitless in the sky. She closed her eyes again, then opened them. At the lip of the dune ahead of her, she saw shadows moving.

Rey started awake, one hand tightening around her staff. She wasn't entirely certain she hadn't been dreaming. She slid forward in the pilot's seat, almost onto her knees on the cockpit floor, using the flight console to conceal herself.

The shadows moved again. Two figures were descending the dune toward the ship. She couldn't quite make them out, and then she saw two more shapes cresting the dune, leading luggabeasts.

Four Teedos coming toward her.

As they drew closer, Rey could make out details. All the Teedos were armed, most of them with staves but one had a rifle. She couldn't see their markings in the darkness, but she didn't need to. They had come either to take the ship or to destroy it. It didn't matter. Either way, Rey wouldn't let them.

The Ghtroc was armed with a fore-mounted dual laser cannon, but the gun was nonoperative. Rey had restored the wiring and firing controls as best she could, but the Tibanna gas required to charge the weapons had long before leaked into the atmosphere and was impossible to replenish. Never mind that using the cannon was a terminal solution, and willing though she was to defend her prize, Rey didn't want to kill anyone if she could avoid it.

Rey rolled from the pilot's chair to the floor and crawled quickly back to the cockpit hallway before getting to her feet. She stumbled through the darkness to the loading ramp, hit the release, and followed it down as it descended, then jumped out before it had touched the ground. Rey ran to the front of the freighter, both hands on her staff. She skidded to a stop, facing the Teedos.

They paused their advance, the nearest of them—the one with the rifle—six, maybe seven meters away. For a long moment nobody moved and nobody spoke. One of the luggabeasts huffed, pawing at the sand, its gears grinding.

"This is mine," Rey said. "It's my ship, do you understand? You can't have it."

The Teedos didn't respond. A deeper darkness had descended. Rey couldn't tell who she was dealing with, scavengers or worse. Her stomach was tight, an ache in the pit of her gut, and she could feel her heart beating in her breast. It was, if anything, colder than before. When she spoke, her breath made clouds of condensation in the air.

"Leave," Rey said. "Go away."

The Teedo nearest her, rifle still lowered, turned his wrapped head to look back at the others. Their bodies were always hidden—everything, including their eyes—so even if the light had been better, Rey wouldn't have been able to read anything in their expressions. The body language was clear enough, though. The Teedo in the lead looked back at her. They had no intention of leaving.

"I don't want to fight," Rey said. "I don't want to fight, but I will. I will."

The Teedo with the rifle brought the weapon up to his shoulder. Six meters was a close-range shot but too far for Rey to cover the distance before he could make it. She figured she had to try, anyway. If she got lucky, if she led with her staff, maybe she would hit the end of the weapon before he fired, maybe she could knock it away, force him to miss. Rey doubted she would be so lucky, but she didn't see any other choice.

She never got the chance to find out.

A blaster bolt zapped into the sand between her and the Teedo with the rifle. The shot was brilliant red in the darkness and made the sand spit and sizzle. A second shot followed the first, hitting closer to the Teedo. Both had come from Rey's right, atop one of the dunes.

"You heard her," Devi said. "It's her ship."

She was standing just over the rise, a small blaster held in both hands. Strunk was beside her, and as Devi spoke, he ran clumsily down the slope, splashing sand as he went. His hands were empty, but he seemed even bigger than before, twice the height of the tallest Teedo.

"I don't have a lot of shots in this thing," Devi said. "But I've got enough left. A couple of you are gonna get really hurt. Or maybe worse."

Strunk had reached the bottom and jogged up alongside Rey. He touched her elbow as he passed but kept moving forward, striding toward the Teedo with the rifle. He reached out and grabbed the weapon by its long barrel, then pulled it aside. The Teedo didn't let go, but he couldn't control where it was pointing. Strunk yanked, and the rifle came out of the Teedo's three-fingered grip. Strunk turned the gun in his hands, found the charging clip, and tore it free. He flung the cartridge over the dunes, then handed the rifle back to the Teedo.

"It's time for you to leave," Devi said.

The Teedos turned and went back the way they had come.

"You're welcome," Devi said, following Rey up the ramp and back into the ship. Strunk's footsteps were heavy on the metal behind them.

"What were you doing out here?" Rey asked. She flicked on the lights in the main compartment and hit the switch to close the ramp once more.

Devi tucked the little blaster into one of her many pockets and ran her grimy fingers through her hair, looking up at Rey. She seemed puzzled.

"We were keeping watch."

"Keeping watch?"

"Yeah, Strunk and I have been camping out here pretty much the last two weeks whenever you headed home." Devi looked genuinely confused. "Someone had to stay on guard, right?"

"Two weeks?"

"About that, yeah. I'd have thought you'd be more grateful."

Rey looked at her staff, then set it against a bulkhead. She didn't know how she should feel. They had been sleeping out in the cold for two weeks, risking the gnaw-jaws and everything else just to guard the ship.

"I didn't know you were doing that," Rey said.

"We've got one of those old emergency shelters we pulled from a wrecked X-wing a couple years ago. It's pretty warm inside, though it gets kinda cozy." Devi shot a grin at Strunk, who was standing mutely by, listening closely. "We normally wait until we see you arrive and then we head out on the salvage runs, get our portions, like that. Hadn't you wondered why you were always here first?"

"I just thought I was early."

"Nah, Rey, we've been making sure everything stays safe."

Rey considered and found that she was struggling with what she should say. It came slowly. "Thank you."

Devi laughed. "See, that's it! You're welcome! It's not a big thing, Rey. We're just protecting our investment, right? That's all it is. Nothing more to it."

Rey nodded slowly.

"So, listen," Devi said. "I was talking with Forna when Forna and Oth and Grand were in Niima the other day, and they say that the *X'us'R'iia* all those months back uncovered an Uulshos XP, one of the yachts, you know? They said it's entirely wrecked, they stripped it of everything, *but* they also said the main engine compartment came down intact. Neither me nor Strunk can ever remember Unkar selling a converter chamber, the thing's just too hard to separate from the remix junction, right? But the one on this XP, it might still be intact. So we're going to go out and take a look, what do you think?"

"I think it's a good idea."

"Gonna be a real pain separating it out, though. Strunk's strong enough to help lift it, but getting it disconnected without making it useless or cracking the diverter, that's the part that's worrying me."

"I can help."

Devi looked surprised. "You sure? It'll leave the ship alone."

"No, I can help," Rey said. "Strunk and I can go. You stay with the ship."

Devi stared at her, then looked away sharply. When she looked back, Rey thought her eyes had grown wet.

"I won't let anyone touch it," Devi promised.

———

It was half a day's ride from the Ghtroc to where Devi said they'd find the Uulshos XP, and Rey drove with Strunk on the back of her speeder. The wreck was almost exactly as Devi had described, broken into six sections that had scattered over a kilometer and a half, with the engines the farthest away. Everything usable had long before been pulled from the cockpit, crew, and passenger areas, and at first look Rey would have said the same thing about the engine room. Whoever had worked the wreck had stripped it down to the bolts.

"What you think?" Strunk asked.

Rey didn't answer at first, ducking beneath a broken crossbeam and stepping into the wreckage. Floor plates had been removed, and the footing was tricky. She brought her flashlight out of her satchel and ran it along the ceiling, then the floor, trying to trace where the power lines had once run to the hyperdrive and finally tracking it back to where the injector complex had once been. She stood for several seconds, taking it all in, then switched off the light and turned to face him.

"I think it'll work," Rey said. "I think we can make it work."

They broke out the tools and began the laborious process of disconnecting the converter from its junction. It took patience and care, because Rey was, in essence, trying to remove a component of the hyperdrive system that had never been designed to be interchangeable. In any other circumstance, it would've been considered safer and much more efficient simply to pull the entire hyperdrive array, right down to the engines, and reinstall a new one. For all the obvious reasons, that wasn't an option. Rey knew she could've managed the physical separation of the chamber from the rest of the engine by herself, but once she'd done so she just as quickly realized she would never have been able to remove it from the ship alone. She simply wasn't strong enough. Strunk could barely handle it himself. Working together, however, they were able to manhandle it off the wreck and get it strapped onto the back of the speeder.

It was after nightfall when they returned to the Ghtroc, finding the lights off and Devi sitting on the lowered loading ramp. She got to her feet when she saw them and pumped a fist triumphantly in the air as they approached. Strunk laughed, and Rey did, too. Working together, they got the component off the speeder and on board the freighter. They shared a dinner, one portion apiece, sitting on the floor, and Devi talked throughout the meal, the way she always seemed to be talking, but Rey found herself enjoying it more that time. When they'd finished, Strunk got up to head for the ramp, Devi moving to follow him.

"See you in the morning, Rey," Devi said and then, to Strunk, "I'll take the first watch."

"You guys can stay on the ship," Rey said. "It's warmer."

They stopped.

"That is true," Devi said. "Also, it doesn't smell so much like Strunk. Which, I hate to say it, that shelter totally does."

"I do not smell." Strunk sounded wounded.

"We *all* smell, Strunk. I can't remember the last time I was in a refresher."

Rey pointed to one of the small closed doors off the main compartment. "Fully functional."

"You serious?"

"No water, but the sonics work."

Devi was already heading for the door. "You can have that first watch, Strunk."

She disappeared into the refresher so quickly Rey couldn't help laughing.

Two days later, Rey flew the Ghtroc 690 light freighter she had found, the spaceship she had spent the better part of a year reassembling, into Niima with Devi sitting in the copilot's seat beside her and Strunk hovering behind them, one of his big hands on the back of each of their chairs. The hyperdrive was functional and communicating cheerfully with the navicomputer. The repulsor engines were humming along at optimal efficiency. The pressure seals on all the external access ways were tight, and the atmosphere was stable, steady, and comfortable. There were only two warning lights flashing on the console, and each was nonessential; one told Rey that the water tanks were empty, and the other told her that the Ghtroc was overdue for its scheduled twenty thousand light-year maintenance.

Devi had roared with laughter when Rey explained what that second light meant.

They flew in from the south, Rey slowing so everyone in Niima could get a good look at the ship as it came in over the airfield. Almost every approach was from the east, and Rey knew that sharp-eyed observers would know the difference, would be wondering who they were and where they had come from. She banked in a lazy loop around the little town, looking through the canopy at the activity below. Devi leaned forward, doing the same. They could see the small figures of scavengers and vendors emerging from their shelters and from beneath awnings, raising hands to shield their eyes from the glare of the sun.

"Think they've seen enough?" Rey asked.

"I think they've never seen anything like this," Devi said.

Rey rolled the ship out of its turn and then, on a whim, gave the engines a sudden nudge. The freighter shot forward, the horizon vanishing from view as she brought the nose up. She turned the ship in a half loop, then rolled out of it and doubled back. Devi whooped. Strunk's grip on the seats tightened. Rey slowed once more as they reacquired the airfield and put the freighter into a hover, letting it turn in place. There was space between the old YT freighter and one of the newer, cleaner ships that Unkar had acquired, and with perfect precision Rey set it down so gently the landing gear didn't make a sound as Jakku once more took the Ghtroc's weight.

She worked the console quickly, excited, putting the ship into standby. Unkar would want to know it worked, that *everything* worked, and when Rey brought him aboard she wanted to be able to show off her work without delay. She released the yoke and got to her feet, Devi and Strunk moving after her. They'd loaded her speeder into the main compartment, and Strunk hit the release for the ramp. As it lowered Rey could see people gathered at the edge of the airfield, trying to get a look at the newcomers.

"Don't let anyone else aboard," Rey told Devi. "Only me and Unkar, nobody else, no matter how much they promise, no matter how hard they beg."

"Ten thousand portions, minimum," Devi said.

"For all of us," Rey said, and she grinned and gunned the speeder forward, down the ramp and out of the airfield, turning hard and fast toward Unkar's place. Someone shouted as she passed, and a couple of the scavengers at the washing station burst into cheers when they saw her, understanding at once just how immense Rey's accomplishment was. She was smiling again, her cheeks aching, but that time she didn't mind so much.

Unkar was waiting outside as she pulled up. He blinked at her slowly, waiting until she'd shut off the speeder and hopped down.

"It's a Ghtroc 690," Rey said. "Fully restored, working hyperdrive, everything but the laser cannon and the water tanks. Everything else fully operational, Unkar."

He blinked at her again, then turned his heavy head to the side, looking toward the airfield. That was when the sound of the engine reached her, and Rey turned to look, as well, just in time to see the Ghtroc rising into the air. It ascended quickly, almost too fast. It banked hard, its nose jerking up. The main engines ignited, and a blue flare of ionized gases jetted from the aft end.

Then the Ghtroc was a dot in the blue sky.

Then it was gone.

Unkar grunted and headed back inside. Rey

heard the outpost coming to life again around her, the voices of scavengers and vendors, Niima returning to normal.

Rey stood there a long time. When she finally moved it was to mount her speeder and drive home, back to the walker. She knew she should be angry, but she wasn't. It took until that night, until she was sitting on her blankets, punching the lenses out of a battered stormtrooper helmet, for her to understand why. It had always been an issue of trust, but never with Devi and Strunk. It had been about trusting herself.

Devi and Strunk had wanted the one thing that Rey absolutely hadn't; they'd even told her so right from the start. But she hadn't listened. She hadn't heard them, because it was the one thing Rey never allowed herself to consider.

They wanted to leave.

But Rey had to stay. At least until they came back for her.

If she left, her parents would have no way of finding her.

She sighed, the sound echoing through the cramped hull that made her home. She shifted over to the workbench, switched the computer on, and loaded her flight simulator. She selected a Ghtroc 720, a suborbital flight with calm atmospheric conditions and no complications.

Rey flew.

But it wasn't the same.

POE

POE DAMERON'S first ship was his mother's RZ-1 A-wing.

It was a good, tight little fighter, much repaired and marked with scars from its years of service. An interceptor, the A-wing had been built for speed rather than strength. Twin-mounted laser canons on either side of the hull spat enough firepower to settle any dogfight—provided the fighter jockey on the stick could gain advantage—and two concussion missile launchers mounted on the fore of the hull could give anything shy of a capital ship a very bad day. It was staggeringly fast at sublight speed. It was more like an armed cockpit with engines stuck to its back than a more traditional fighter, hyperresponsive and overpowered and meant to be flown solo, without copilot or astromech support.

The A-wing had been part of his mother's compensation package when Poe's parents mustered out of the Rebellion some six months after the Battle of Endor, and it went with them to their new home in the fledgling colony on Yavin 4. She'd continued to fly it for a couple of years after, mostly in civilian defense, and every so often she would take Poe up in it. He would sit on her lap inside the cramped cockpit, his hands on the stick and her hands on his, and he could feel the ship answering their control. He could feel them moving through the air, the atmosphere pushing against them, the pull of gravity trying to refuse them.

Then they would break through the thin skin that protected the moon they called their home, and the Yavin gas giant would suddenly glow that much brighter against the darkness of space. All the push and pull of atmosphere and gravity would vanish, and it was as close to perfection as young Poe could imagine. He would stare up through the canopy and lose track of the stars and feel the freedom and the potential, that he could go anywhere, that he could do anything. That was when he knew that whatever else he would be, he would be a pilot.

His mother had flown in the Battle of Endor, had taken part in the massive fleet action against the second Death Star while Poe's father had pounded the ground alongside his fellow Pathfinder commandos on the forest moon below. She didn't like to talk about her service, but Poe knew that much, and when he had asked for more information, she had gently refused or redirected him. It was enough, she told Poe, that she had done her duty, that she had answered when called. *That* she had was more important, she said, than *what* she had done.

"People were hurting," his mother told him. "People were suffering. Your father and I couldn't sit and do nothing."

It wasn't until years later, long after she had passed away and Poe had entered the New Republic's service and become a pilot himself, that he began to learn the true scope of her heroism—that Lieutenant Shara Bey had been awarded the Bronze Nova for Conspicuous Gallantry during the Liberation of Gorma; that she had earned her triple ace less than a week later, during Operation: Mynock Bite, raiding the Imperial fuel depot at Beroq 4; that she had flown in dozens of other battles, skirmishes, and actions; that her file held countless testimonies from fellow pilots, praising her skill, claiming that they owed Poe Dameron's mother their lives.

Poe's father was more forthcoming with war stories, though he would never talk about his own actions, instead focusing on the heroism and bravery of others. He'd tell Poe how General Solo was the best shot he'd ever seen with a blaster; or about the time when one of his squadmates had gotten them out of an ambush with a rewired comlink and two chargers from a standard-issue rebreather; or about the time his squad had been assaulting an ISB base in the Outer Rim and no one had known how to get inside until, completely by accident, they had taken down an AT-ST that then crashed into the base and allowed them easy access.

"Did you ever get scared?" Poe had asked his father once, when he was nine. It had been a year since his mother had passed. Up until then, Poe had been able to imagine dogfights as pristine, glowing, spectacular displays of light and speed and grace and wit. He'd imagined stormtroopers as empty suits of armor, not as the men and women within. Losing his mother had brought death to him in a way he never could've conceived of before, and he understood then that war was not romantic; people died, and the dead were not returned to those who loved them, no matter how much they might wish otherwise.

That was as terrifying a thought as it was a heartbreaking one.

They had been out on the edge of their property, the little ranch his parents had built after settling on Yavin 4. It was late afternoon and the sounds coming out of the jungle always got louder and more ominous as the night approached. His father had been repairing one of the generators on the perimeter fence, and Poe was helping him with the work. They'd worked in silence, much as they had passed many of the days since Poe's mother had died, united in their shared grief.

So Poe had been surprised that his father had answered, surprised that his father had known exactly what he was referring to.

"Was I ever scared?" His father studied the dynamic hammer he was holding, the tool still vibrating, making its strange singsong moan as it resonated. He switched it off and dropped it into the toolbox at Poe's feet. He wiped his hands on his pants and squinted into the jungle. Overhead, the sun was slipping behind the Yavin gas giant, casting the world in a ruby hue.

"When I was on the ground, back at Endor, there was this moment when the bucketheads had us," his father said. "We'd been surrounded by stormtroopers, all of us, caught. I thought we were done, I thought we had lost, and I mean everything. The war, everything. I looked up, past trees taller than these, into this perfect blue sky. You could just barely see the Death Star in the daytime. I knew what was happening up there, the battle they were fighting."

His father smiled at him, a sad smile.

"And I thought that your mother was looking down on me, right then. In the middle of whatever she was doing, whatever fight she was fighting, it was like I could feel her eyes on me. I could feel how much she loved me, and how much she loved you."

He wiped his hands again and plucked another tool from the box, returning his attention to the fence.

He checked his scanner and took another look at the utter emptiness of space surrounding him. There were three other T-85 Incom-FreiTek X-wings with him and BB-8, flying a finger-four formation. This was Rapier Squadron, *his* squadron, his command.

"All wings, report in," Poe said.

"Rapier Two." Lieutenant Karé Kun sounded positively bored. "Everything's green, Commander."

"Rapier Three, and I have to agree with Rapier Two, Commander." This was Iolo Arana, flying to Poe's withdrawn starboard. "This is another waste of fuel and time."

"Rapier Four. Standing by."

"You see," said Poe, "you should all follow Muran's example, there. You hear how nicely Rapier Four reported in, without editorializing or anything?"

The sound of Karé's yawning for effect came over Poe's speakers. He grinned, despite himself.

"Bring it around to one-four mark four," Poe said. "One last loop and then we're back to base."

The formation banked as one, each fighter executing the turn in rapid sequence, following

"Thing was, I was *worried*, but I wasn't *scared*."

"So you were *never* scared?"

His father laughed softly. "I didn't say that. I'm saying that what I was afraid of then isn't what scares me now."

"What're you afraid of now?"

Poe watched his father raise his eyes from the fence and stare up into the dusk sky. The sun had almost slipped behind the gas giant, and in the last moments of daylight everything seemed oddly brighter, more sharply in focus.

"That it was all for nothing," his father said.

BB-8, secure in the astromech socket behind the cockpit of Poe's X-wing, burbled a question. Plugged into the fighter, the droid's binary-speak was automatically decoded and displayed on the console, but Poe didn't actually need to read the translation to understand what the droid was asking. He grinned and reached over his left shoulder to tweak one of the knobs that controlled the power to the port-side engines, adjusting the flow rate to the dorsal of the two fusial thrusters.

"Just talking to myself, Beebee-Ate," Poe said. "Just wandering down memory lane."

Rapier One's lead. BB-8 burbled again, less communicating than talking to himself, and Poe wondered what the little machine was computing. Every droid had its own manifest personality, and most that he'd encountered were predictable to certain stereotypes—bossy, sullen, grumpy— within their respective programming. BB-8 was his own case, sometimes childlike, sometimes precocious, but every now and then Poe wondered if the droid wasn't daydreaming, which was absurd, of course, because that would imply BB-8 had an active imagination.

Iolo broke into his thoughts, grumbling over the comms. "Thing I don't understand, Commander, is why we keep coming out here."

"We are members of the New Republic's navy," Poe said. "Or have you forgotten who it is you signed up to protect?"

"I know it's our *job*. What I'm saying is, look, I understand the Republic is concerned about piracy in the trade lanes, I get that. I absolutely, totally, I *get* it. Impact to galactic commerce, citizens need to feel safe, rule of law, all of that. But we've been flying this patrol for three weeks now—"

"Four," Karé corrected.

"Four—thank you, Karé—and not one smuggler, not one pirate, not one miscreant, heck, not even one unmanned drone has so much as beeped our scanners. I'd take a hunk of space debris. Anything."

"What do you want me to tell you, Iolo?" Poe asked. "I've been writing to the Guavians daily asking them to step up their criminal activities, but so far, they're just not responding."

"That's your problem," Karé said. "The Guavians can't *read*, Poe. You should be writing to the Hutts."

Laughter filled his cockpit, even Muran joining in, and Poe found himself grinning and shaking his head, and then BB-8 was chirping and beeping excitedly. Poe checked his scanner, then tweaked the gain, straightening up against the flight couch.

"Got something," he said.

The laughter ended abruptly.

"Beebee-Ate, patch it to the squadron."

There was a chirp in response, a blast of static, and then a strained voice, oddly modulated—or someone speaking through a rebreather—filled the cockpit.

"—*free trader* Yissira Zyde—*nder attack, please, to any vessel receivi—us we—*"

"Beebee-Ate, get me a fix, transmit to all Rapiers."

The display on the console came alive. The map of their patrol sector flickered to the Mirrin sector.

"—*have—st power to sub—ght engines cannot man—peat cannot maneuver—multiple—ighters attacking—*"

Poe's heartbeat quickened as he looked at the map, watching as BB-8 continued to isolate the distress call. There was no point in telling the droid to work faster; the astromech was working as quickly as he could, computing with all his power, but still Poe couldn't fight his rising anxiety, the urge to move, to move now, even if there was no place yet to go. Lines crisscrossed the map, zooming in, tighter and tighter.

BB-8 emitted a triumphant chirp.

"Got it," Poe said. "Suraz 4. All Rapiers, confirm hyperspace coordinates."

Almost immediately, Rapier Two confirmed, followed by Rapier Four, then Rapier Three.

"We're going in hot," Poe said. "Punch it."

They came out of lightspeed one after the other, with what Poe's map told him was Suraz 5 dead ahead of them.

"Lock S-foils in attack position," Poe said. "All Rapiers, report in."

"Rapier Two, standing by."

"Rapier Three, standing by."

"Rapier Four, standing by."

"Accelerate and stay tight." Poe rebalanced power and nudged the stick forward, dipping his X-wing's nose as he felt the stability foils on the fighter rise then settle into combat position. The fighter accelerated at his command, surging forward as if shoved suddenly from behind, the motion itself bringing back the memory of his mother, of flying with her in her A-wing. The new T-85s were as fast and agile as anything she had flown back in the day, and not for the first time, Poe wished she had lived to see them, to see him leading his own squadron.

"*Yissira Zyde*," Poe said. "This is Commander Poe Dameron of the Republic Navy, we have received your distress call and are en route to render assistance."

Nothing came back.

Still in formation, the X-wings broke around Suraz 5, now heading at attack speed for Suraz 4. Poe imagined pirates, and assumed the engagement would be a short one. Most of the criminal organizations working the trade lanes of the Mirrin sector were poorly financed, using ships that were held together more by force of will than anything approaching engineering. Four X-wings would normally be enough to scare anyone off. That's what he imagined. That's what he expected.

It wasn't what they encountered.

"Caraya's soul," Rapier Two's voice was breathless and sounded almost hollow as it came over the cockpit speakers.

The freighter, presumably the *Yissira Zyde*, listed in space, venting atmosphere from a hull breach on its starboard side, a cloud of debris mixing with the evaporating air. Even as they closed in, Poe could see the tiny figures of the boarding party leaving the attack shuttles that had pulled alongside, the glow of repulsor-powered jetpacks moving shining white figures across the emptiness of the vacuum to enter the crippled ship. Better equipped, better armed, the boarding parties and the shuttles both, and that told Poe everything he needed to know, even before he saw the TIEs coming about, eight of them, moving to intercept Rapier Squadron.

"First Order," Poe said. "Break, two elements, Rapier Two, tight on me."

"On you tight, Rapier Leader."

"Rapier Three, you and Four see if you can't get those shuttles to break off."

"Confirmed," Iolo said.

"Two against eight, boss," Karé said.

"Yeah," Poe said. "I feel kinda bad for them."

He heard her laugh, and then they were into it.

There was a moment when Poe was sure they would pull it off, that they would send the First Order packing and rescue the freighter. He lined up his first shot on approach and put his X-wing into a corkscrew as the first blasts from the TIEs lanced past, missing him and Rapier Two altogether. He pulled the trigger and the four laser cannons fired in two tandem blasts. The lead TIE cracked, then flared, then just wasn't there anymore. He broke to his right, yanking back on the stick. BB-8 sang a burst of binary, and then Poe was behind a second TIE. The enemy fighter jinked left and Poe saw it coming. When the TIE corrected, trying to cut to the starboard instead, it crossed dead center in his field of fire, and it was two down, just like that.

Then Karé came up from beneath another, and instead of eight TIEs, there were five left, and Rapier Three and Four had broken through the fighter screen. From his cockpit, Poe could see them both opening fire on the first of the two shuttles, could see the blasts crackle and dissipate against the First Order shields. Both shuttles immediately broke station, one heading high and the other low, and Poe figured they were making a run for it.

Two of the TIEs had picked him up, zigzagging as he tried to shake them. They fired, blasts passing harmlessly, but they didn't stop and they didn't relent. BB-8 whimpered, worried.

"It's nothing," Poe assured him.

BB-8 made a noise that, Poe thought, sounded decidedly unconvinced.

He rebalanced power, boosting his forward deflectors, still weaving, dipping, jerking to deny the pursuing fighters their shot. He reached over his shoulder again for the flow regulators, closing both of his starboard engines to a trickle in an instant, then yanked the stick hard to port. The X-wing wheeled, and the straps holding Poe to his seat dug into his shoulders, but then his nose was toward them. Two of their shots hit and sizzled against his shields, and he was firing again.

Then there were three TIEs left, and then there were two as Rapier Two blasted her second. Poe restored his starboard engines and checked on the position of the shuttles in time to watch as Rapier Three and Four destroyed one of them. He watched as the second seemed to stand motionless in space for an instant, then stretch before snapping into hyperspace. The remaining TIEs split their formation, each now fleeing, and Poe swept in behind one as Rapier Two crossed overhead pursuing the other. Then there were two more fireballs. Poe looped back around, scanning for any other vessels, and from the corner of his eye, he saw a glow begin to rise from the stern of *Yissira Zyde*.

"Muran! Iolo! Break port!" he shouted.

Rapier Three banked sharply, high and left, but Muran went left and low, and it wasn't enough, and it wasn't in time. The freighter stretched and snapped out of realspace, the wake of its jump to lightspeed buffeting Rapier Four's X-wing, shearing first the upper, then the lower of its starboard S-foils from its hull.

"Muran!" Karé shouted. "Muran, eject!"

Rapier Four exploded.

"It's unfortunate," Major Lonno Deso said. "It's never easy to lose one of your squadron, Commander. But I've reviewed the flight data, I've reviewed the entire engagement up to and including the astromech telemetry, and there's nothing you could have done. Lieutenant Muran's death is tragic, but it's my considered opinion it was unavoidable."

"I disagree," said Poe.

"You can't blame yourself."

The sympathy in Deso's voice and expression were unmistakable, so much so that Poe felt a sharp, almost hot spur of anger in his breast. He clenched his fists, unclenched them, then looked past Deso at the wall of the briefing room behind him. A display showed the galaxy, color overlays marking realms of political influence. Their position at the Republic base in Mirrin Prime was marked by a gently pulsing gold dot at sea in the royal blue that represented the New Republic's sphere of influence. It stretched far and wide, from the Inner Core to great swaths of the Outer Rim. A gray band designated the neutral region of the Borderland, and beyond that was a pocket of crimson, First Order territory.

For the first time, Poe saw the map and thought it was lying.

"I don't blame myself," Poe said. He looked at Major Deso pointedly. "I'm blaming the First Order."

"Commander." Deso sighed. "We are not having this discussion again."

"This isn't another isolated incident, Lonno. I'm seeing the same intelligence reports that you are."

"The Senate Intelligence Committee has reviewed the reports and has found them inconclusive, at best grossly overstated, Poe. This is a non-issue. It's a big galaxy. The First Order is a remnant born of a war thirty years gone.

Yes, they persist, yes, they continue, but by all accounts they do so barely. They are, at best, an ill-organized, poorly equipped, and badly funded group of loyalists who use propaganda and fear to inflate their strength and their importance."

"They're flying state-of-the-art TIEs, they're using commando boarding parties and latest-generation attack shuttles in clear violation of the Galactic Concordance." Poe leaned forward, pressing his index finger into the table. Deso raised an eyebrow, looking at the offending digit, then at Poe. Poe went on. "They're training troops and pilots. We interrupted a military operation, Lonno, not some snatch and grab. They wanted the *Yissira Zyde* and they got it. They wanted it badly enough they paid for it with eight TIEs, those pilots, and however many people were aboard the shuttle that Muran and Iolo shot down. That's not a poorly organized force. That's not a poorly *motivated* force. That's a real threat."

"An emerging threat, then, Commander Dameron."

Poe straightened, returning his hand to his side. "Give it to the Resistance."

Deso scowled, as if Poe had just offered him

a particularly bitter piece of fruit. "Don't be absurd. The Resistance is as overstated as the First Order."

"They're at least doing something about them!"

"*Rumored* to be doing something about them," Deso said.

"We have to act."

Major Deso cleared his throat. "I'll pass along your concerns to Command."

"That's not enough. We need to know what the *Yissira Zyde* was hauling. We need to know why they took it and, more importantly, where. I'd like permission to take the Rapiers out, try to track the trajectory, see if we can't find the freighter."

"Denied."

"There are questions—"

"I said denied, Commander. Rapier is assigned Mirrin sector patrol, that's all. Your orders are to continue as before. Nothing more, and nothing less." Deso cocked his head as if trying to watch the words enter Poe's ears. "Am I clear?"

Poe tried again. "It's going to happen again, you realize that, don't you?"

"If it does, it'll be dealt with then."

"So we do nothing? That's the solution? An emerging threat, and we do nothing?"

"That is correct."

"That is insane," Poe said.

Deso opened his mouth, then thought better of what he was about to say. He sighed and went around the table to stand by Poe's side. When he spoke next, his tone was much more subdued. "I don't like it, either, but this is the order from Republic Command, do you understand? We don't engage the First Order, we don't provoke the First Order. I don't like it any more than you do, but those are *orders*, Commander. You break them, you'll be up on charges. You'll lose your commission."

"It's going to happen again," Poe repeated.

"Then we'll respond when the time comes."

Poe shook his head. That wasn't what he'd meant. He was thinking of his father.

Thinking of what had made his father afraid that day fixing the fence on Yavin 4.

His X-wing stood unattended in the hangar bay, parked beside Rapier Two's and Rapier Three's. The space for Rapier Four's was painfully empty, just an oblong oil stain on the floor where a coolant leak had stained the permacrete.

Poe stared at the empty space for several seconds before turning his attention to his own fighter, walking around it slowly, taking his time. BB-8 rolled along behind him, chirping to himself. Beneath the hangar lights, the paint job looked tarnished, in need of a touch-up. The black base over the majority of the fuselage was weathered, scraped by micrometeorite impacts and atmospheric burns, washed out to almost a deep gray. The flight markings, in orange, were similarly distressed. He set a hand against the side of the X-wing's nose, felt the metal of the hull cool and solid beneath his palm. The ship had made it through combat without a fleck of damage, as solid and ready and sure as ever.

He'd seen his mother doing the same thing, he remembered. Long after she'd given up the flight stick, her A-wing parked between the storage units on the ranch, she'd still walk around that fighter, occasionally touching the ship here or there, as if to reassure it, or to reassure herself. Remembering what she had done to stop the Empire, maybe. Remembering what she had been willing to sacrifice.

"We finishing this?" Karé's voice carried through the near-empty hangar.

Poe turned and saw her standing with Iolo, just inside the doors from the pilot's prep room. Both were wearing their flight suits, their helmets in hand. Their respective astromechs waited patiently at their sides, an old R4 unit that Karé had trusted her life to for as long as Poe had known her and an R5 model that Iolo had only acquired in the last six weeks.

Poe shook his head.

"They took that freighter somewhere, Commander." Iolo looked down at his R5 unit and nudged it with the toe of his boot. The droid rolled a couple of centimeters, then rolled back, emitting a sound that Poe took for the binary equivalent of a confirmation. They were in this together. Iolo looked at him with his oddly colored eyes. He was Keshian, in almost all appearances identical to human, but for whatever reason of nature his people perceived through a broader visual spectrum, from the ultraviolet into the infrared. It made him deadly in a dogfight, able to pick out ships or objects that Poe couldn't see with his naked eyes.

Karé was human, her hair pleated and bound

in an elaborate series of braids. Another colonist, like Poe, she was what was referred to as a "victory kid," one of the hundreds of millions—if not billions—of sentients who had been conceived in response to the Empire's fall. Poe wondered sometimes how many beings had chosen not to have children while Palpatine lived, how many had thought bringing a child into the Emperor's galaxy would be not a blessing but a curse.

"Figure we need to find out where," Karé said. "We owe it to Muran, right?"

"No go," Poe said. "By Major Deso's order."

"What?" Iolo said.

Karé turned. "Let's just see about that."

"Karé, don't," Poe said. "It's not his call. It's coming down from on high."

She faced him again, suspicious. "'On high' who?"

"He won't say, other than Command. It could be Senate level. We go up on anything other than a routine patrol, we're all looking at charges."

Iolo's mouth tightened, corners edging down in a frown. He glanced at Karé, then back to Poe.

"So what're we doing, Poe? We're just sitting on our hands?"

"No," Poe said. "We're going on patrol."

He waited until they were out of Mirrin Prime and beyond the edge of the system before he keyed his comm.

"Rapier Two, Rapier Three," he said. "Comlink your astromechs to Rapier One and upload all telemetry from the Suraz engagement to Beebee-Ate, please."

He heard Karé laugh softly. "Oh, you are slick, Poe."

Iolo needed a second longer, then said, "We're doing this?"

"*I'm* doing this," Poe said. "Not going to let you both flush your careers on a disobedience charge. If someone is going to take a fall for this, let it be me. I'm not planning to be gone long, anyway. This is just recon. Everything goes well, I'll be back before Deso knows we ever split up."

BB-8 beeped, then launched into a long song of chirps and beeps.

"Your droid sounds happy," Karé said.

"He's got a trajectory on the *Yissira Zyde's* hyperspace jump." Poe checked the map and frowned. There was nothing on the jump path that made sense to him, nothing habitable or even remotely so. It was more than possible that the First Order troops who had stolen the freighter had plotted multiple jumps, he realized, altering their direction and flight path, conceivably even doubling back on it. "This may be a wild mynock hunt."

"But it may not be," Iolo said.

"Don't sound so somber, Rapier Three."

"We're already down one good pilot," Iolo said. "And I don't think Karé is particularly looking for a field promotion to Rapier One."

"Copy that," Karé agreed. "Be smart, Poe, and hurry back, okay?"

Poe guided the X-wing out of formation as BB-8 continued to plot the coordinates for the hyperspace jump. "You know it."

"Hey, Rapier One?"

"Go ahead, Rapier Two."

"May the Force be with you."

Poe grinned, and then realspace vanished and he was in the tunnel.

The *Yissira Zyde* was an *NK-Witell*-class freighter, BB-8 informed Poe. Built by Sanhar-Witell, the ship required a minimum crew of two, but had accommodations for a total of twelve passengers. Properly configured, the ship could haul seventy-five metric tons of cargo, though it more commonly maxed out at fifty metric tons. Faster-than-light travel was achieved through the use of the Sanhar model 67 hyperdrive, rated at class three, with sublight travel provided by the venerable Hoersch-Kessel model alpha. The class, BB-8 went on to tell him, entered common service some seventeen years before, and at present there were estimated to be 137,417 still in use throughout the trade lanes that ran from—

"Thank you, Beebee-Ate, think I've got it," Poe said.

The droid beeped, unperturbed. Without Poe's asking, a new flow of data much more pertinent to his interests scrolled across the console. The *Yissira Zyde's* last stop prior to the hijacking had been at the commerce center on Mennar-Daye, where it had been subjected to a thorough screening by Republic authorities before taking on new cargo. That cargo consisted of forty-six high-capacity charging arrays, the kind used for energy discharge augmentation and easily adaptable to military use in, say, shipboard turbolasers. The ship's next port of call would have been in the corporate sector, and presumably the transaction was aboveboard, though Poe wondered if the whole thing hadn't been a setup by the First Order from the start. Comparing the flight range of the *NK-Witell* class and further tracking back the *Yissira Zyde's* logged itinerary, BB-8 was able to estimate its remaining fuel at the time of the First Order hijacking. This produced a maximum range on its hyperspace route, provided—of course, that the freighter hadn't dropped back into realspace to alter direction, in which case . . .

"In which case we're shot, yes, I get it."

Given all this, BB-8 told Poe, there were seven possible systems where the freighter could have exited hyperspace—again presuming direct line of travel—before exhausting its fuel supply. The X-wing itself had enough range to hit five of these destinations before reaching the point of no return.

"Let's do them in order," Poe told BB-8.

It was the third stop, and Poe almost skipped it, because there was quite literally *nothing* of interest on the galactic charts for its position. But if his mother had taught him to fly and to love it, his father had taught him that when you commit to doing something, you commit to going all the way or don't do it at all, and so Poe brought them snapping back into realspace in a system so desolate the scouts who'd discovered it hadn't bothered to even give it a name, just an alphanumeric designation: OR-Kappa-2722.

The first thing that happened when the stars returned and the X-wing settled back into proper space-time was that BB-8 screamed. It was a surprising noise, and it made Poe jump in his seat. It wasn't a scream of pain—Poe had heard those before, found the death cry of an astromech particularly heartrending—and it wasn't the gleeful, rapid-fire babble of droid triumph spoken in binary. It was a sound of shock, as if BB-8 had turned a corner expecting to find an empty room and had, instead, run into a rancor den.

Which, Poe reasoned, wasn't actually a bad analogy for where they now found themselves.

"Well, at least it's not the *whole* fleet," he heard himself say. It had sounded funnier in his head.

There were—and this was on the basis of what he could see, though later he was pleased that the flight computer had almost entirely agreed with his initial assessment—three Star Destroyers, one of them *Imperial* class; four frigates, two of them venerable *Lancer* class; two Maxima-A heavy cruisers; and one *Dissident*-class light cruiser. This did not include the array of smaller vessels that seemed to swarm around the fleet, everything from unmanned repair drones and droids to what, at first count, Poe took to be seventy-plus TIE fighters.

BB-8 squeaked a question.

"Not yet," Poe said. "Can you find the *Yissira Zyde*? Do you see it?"

BB-8 beeped and whimpered.

"Well, we've come all this way. I think we ought to leave with something."

A mournful whine. Another question, just a slight, soft chirp.

Ahead of them, somewhere between the nearest Star Destroyer and the first of the heavy cruisers, roughly two dozen TIE fighters wheeled around at once. There was something oddly beautiful in the maneuver, the sheer number of fighters swinging to their new heading together. Poe remembered watching flocks of whisper birds, the way they would bank and swoop in silent unison over the jungle on Yavin 4.

"Yes, Beebee-Ate," Poe said. "I think they've seen us."

The one thing they had going for them, at least at the beginning, was the element of surprise. Not the surprise of an X-wing appearing in the middle of a First Order staging point—though Poe did take a certain amount of pleasure from the thought of the chaos his arrival must've caused on the many and varied bridges of the vessels before him—but rather the surprise of what he and BB-8 did next.

They charged.

BB-8 whirred.

"Yeah, I think boosting the front deflectors is a good idea, too," Poe told him. "And power down the weapons, divert to engines."

BB-8 beeped, agreeing that this was a very good idea given a very bad situation.

"Just until we find it," Poe said. "Just until we have proof."

Then Commander Poe Dameron didn't have much more to say, because he was too busy trying to keep them both alive. He corkscrewed right off the bat, deploying his S-foils as he did before

breaking hard to starboard and then, almost immediately, looping into a tight Corellian end-over that brought him nose first into the midst of the onrushing TIEs. They scattered to his sides, twisting in their flight to come around on his tail, and several opened fire.

It was a mistake on their part. They'd been overzealous coming after him, smelling blood in the water, eager to feast on the lone X-wing. But there were too many TIEs in pursuit, and the first salvo of shots proved the point as two of the TIEs were clipped by friendly fire, sending them spinning in out-of-control arcs, while another three or four—it was hard for Poe to keep track and stay alive at the same time—failed to avoid collisions. The explosions flared behind him as he jinked again, pulling up sharply into a rapid displacement roll that brought him in range of the nearest of the frigates. The enemy ship opened fire at once, and the TIEs at Poe's back again scattered, desperate to avoid being hit by their own allied vessel. The X-wing rocked, then dipped abruptly as a blast glanced off the forward deflectors, but the shields dropped out of green only for a second, and Poe still had control.

"Tell me you see it, Beebee-Ate," Poe muttered. The droid didn't answer. Now the X-wing was so close to the frigate that Poe could swear he was seeing stormtroopers and First Order officers staring at him through the portholes as he raced past. The firing from the frigate stopped. Someone on a command deck somewhere had wisely ordered the capital ships to keep their guns silent for fear of tearing one another to pieces.

Poe brought the X-wing through a wingover, crossed the ventral axis of the frigate, and without needing to ask for it felt as much as saw BB-8 redistributing the fighter's power, shield balanced again and a new rush to the engines. The fighter rolled, corrected, and began climbing with its nose to the belly of one of the Star Destroyers.

BB-8 whistled a warning.

"Yes, I know they have tractor beams," Poe said. "Have you found it?"

There was a pause, long enough for Poe to realize that the TIEs were once more closing in, and closing in quickly if somewhat more judiciously. Laser cannon fire burned through space around him, buffeting the X-wing.

From behind him, BB-8 emitted a song

of triumph, and Poe glanced to the display for a fraction of a second, long enough to see the word *transponder* being translated from the droid's binary-speak.

"Outstanding," Poe said. "Get us a jump out of here!"

Two of the TIEs had come in, flanking his X-wing, preparing to sandwich him, and now he saw another three locking on to his tail, covering the angles of his turn. He was running out of options and time.

"Hurrying would be really good, Beebee-Ate."

The droid burbled and then advised he change heading to one-zero mark two.

"Hold on," Poe said, checking his flanks. The TIEs on his tail were firing, almost herding him. He had one maneuver left that he could think of, one his mother had told him she'd seen one other pilot do, only once, and that in atmosphere. A L'ullo Stand, she'd called it. Doing it in a vacuum, in zero gravity, Poe had no idea if it would work.

He cut thrust to the engines, yanking the stick back a fraction of a second after. The X-wing's nose snapped up sharply, still racing on its current heading. In atmosphere, wind resistance and gravity would slow the fighter down, theoretically forcing the pursuing attackers to overshoot. Out of atmosphere, the deceleration would be negligible without the aid of counterthrust.

Nose up, Poe kicked his engines to life again, rolling the fighter in a one-eighty and slamming the X-wing nose-down once more. He was, for the moment, flying backward as quickly as he'd been flying forward, above the attacking TIEs. Another salvo ripped beneath his ship as the enemy tried to track his move.

"Power," he told BB-8.

The laser cannons came alive as the main thrust returned, and Poe opened fire immediately. The first of the TIEs had seen the maneuver coming, breaking hard starboard and descending, but that had left the remaining two exposed. The X-wing's shots cut through the darkness, glowing bolts that hit first one fighter, then the next. The TIEs tumbled, the lead now bucking up, fins colliding with fins, cockpit balls crushing one another. Debris exploded, and Poe wrenched the stick, pulling into a spiral to avoid the remnants of the collision. BB-8 all but shouted at him that they were now on the proper heading, and Poe Dameron leveled the nose and punched the hyperdrive activator. The last thing he saw as they entered hyperspace was the shots of the pursuing TIE fighters, left light-years behind them.

Iolo and Karé weren't on station when he came out of lightspeed on the edge of the Mirrin system and adjusted his heading to Mirrin Prime. BB-8 burbled, pleased with himself; the *Yissira Zyde's* transponder signal had been clear and strong, and while they'd traveled through hyperspace the droid had been able to review the flight data collected during the engagement. BB-8 had located the freighter aboard the second of the three Star Destroyers. The mission, as far as Poe was concerned, had been successful.

Any sense of triumph was stifled when Mirrin Control came online during his approach.

"Rapier One, this is Mirrin Flight, respond."

The voice was male, older, and Poe didn't recognize it. "Rapier One."

"Approach landing bay twenty-two, you are cleared for landing."

"Mirrin Flight, Rapier Squadron berths bay seven, confirm please."

"Commander Poe Dameron?"

"That's correct," Poe said.

"You are directed to bay twenty-two. Do not deviate your approach. Mirrin Flight out."

The comm went silent. Behind Poe, BB-8 tweeted mournfully.

"Yeah," Poe agreed. "We're in trouble."

Bay twenty-two was empty when Poe brought the X-wing in to land, shutting down the repulsors as the fighter settled on its landing gear. He powered down the ship's systems, considered letting the engines remain on low-power standby for a moment, and then decided there wasn't any point. If he was about to be arrested, if he was looking at a court-martial, he wasn't going to try to run. He'd face the consequences of his actions, and he'd defend them as the right ones. He popped the cockpit and tried to enjoy the first breath of nonrecycled air that he'd had in hours. The cockpit always developed a funk after a long flight, worse after combat, with the combination of electrics and heated metals and his own sweat. There'd been times when he would emerge from his cockpit to find his flight suit soaked with his own perspiration, feeling as wrung out and

exhausted as if he'd been running a footrace for hours. The physical and mental stress of fighter combat always took a toll.

He keyed the release for BB-8, freeing the droid from his socket, then unfastened his helmet and removed his gloves. The bay remained empty, peculiarly so, the doors into it closed. It was very odd. Even in a disused landing bay, you could always find something—power couplings left along a wall, or cabling coiled in a corner, or bits and pieces of replacement parts or spare ordnance. Something.

There was nothing there, as if the bay had been swept clean, as if it had been sterilized.

Poe hit the quick release on his harness, then vaulted over the lip of the cockpit, dropping straight to the floor without bothering to use the handholds. The sound of his boots hitting the ground echoed in the empty space. He felt BB-8 pressing against the back of his calf, heard him whistle softly.

The doors to the bay opened and three figures entered, striding toward him. The one in the middle, in the lead, looked to be in his late fifties, perhaps older, a human male wearing a Republic military uniform. The other two

were unmistakably shore police, a short-horned Devaronian and a human female. They had their sidearms holstered, but they had the look, too, that they were expecting trouble and that they wouldn't put up with it if they found it.

The man in the lead stopped some two meters from Poe and BB-8, then looked him up and down quickly. He had a rank cluster at his collar marking him as a major. Poe had never seen him before.

"Commander Dameron?"

"You are?"

"Major Ematt. You'll come with us, please."

"I've got a report I need to file with Major Deso. We located the *Yissira Zyde*."

"Major Deso is occupied." The man, Ematt, turned back to the door and began walking at once, fully expecting Poe to follow him. The two shore police waited.

Poe followed, BB-8 rolling along behind him.

There was a speeder, a low-slung standard military ride, waiting for them outside. The human shore police officer drove, Major Ematt seated beside her. The Devaronian sat with Poe in the back, BB-8 on the floor between them. The

droid was oddly silent, but the central black lens on his half-domed head rotated between Poe and the Devaronian several times, as if trying to understand what was going on there. Poe could sympathize. He leaned forward.

"Am I under arrest?" he asked Ematt.

"Do you want to be?"

"Where's the rest of my squadron? Lieutenant Kun and Lieutenant Arana?"

"They're being dealt with."

Poe didn't like the sound of that.

The speeder slowed at a corner, then accelerated out of the turn, and they were out of the airfield portion of the Mirrin base, skimming across the tarmac that separated the fighter groups from the main buildings. The sky above was gray, warning of a storm, and beyond the edges of the base Poe could see the mountains and the shimmer of rainfall in the distance. The weather could change fast, and he wondered if they'd be under cover before the storm reached them. The wind was already picking up.

They weren't heading for the main base, but instead for a collection of prefabs that had been recently erected on the north side. The storm

broke over them as they came to a stop, sheets of cold rain that covered the ground at once, making puddles of water that rippled and spread away from the repulsors as the speeder floated in place. Ematt got out, already soaked, and waited for BB-8 and Poe to follow him. Poe hesitated, trying to read the situation. Something in Ematt's manner, his bearing, reminded Poe of his father, and Poe saw it, suddenly: Ematt and Deso may have shared a rank, but Ematt, like Poe's father, was a veteran. He had seen war, and had seen too much of it.

Poe exited the speeder, BB-8 rolling out behind him and hitting the pavement with a soft thump and a gentle splash. The speeder pulled away. Ematt led them to the farthest of the huts and pressed his palm to the security plate on the door. There was a beep as his identity was verified, then the sound of locks sliding back, and the door slid open.

"Go on in," Ematt said. "Your droid and I will wait out here."

Poe nodded, still unsure. He stepped through the door, and it closed immediately behind him.

He entered a repurposed briefing room,

minimalist, with perhaps two dozen chairs and a desk, but on the far side of the hut someone had placed a cot and a trunk, so it had the appearance of both office and barracks. A holoprojector, used for analysis and planning, glowed in an opposite corner, projecting one of the Republic news feeds, but it had been muted, making it seem as if the reporter were speaking in pantomime. On the far wall, opposite where he'd entered, were two displays showing the galaxy, similar to the overlay map in Deso's office. It took Poe another second to realize the difference, that these weren't political maps but rather operational ones, showing troop and fleet movements.

There was a woman at the desk, her head down, working with a datapad. Poe waited, aware he was dripping water on the floor. He realized he was still holding his flight helmet and felt slightly foolish, so he set it down on the seat of one of the empty chairs, and when he straightened up again the woman had risen and was looking at him intently, as if she could see not through him but rather *into* him. She was older than Ematt, with braided hair pinned tightly in place. She was short, but that was only her height, not her stature. Something about her didn't seem just to fill the space but to *command* it. She was in uniform, but it wasn't Republic, not quite. It looked as if it had started that way and then, at some point, turned in favor of serviceable rather than ceremonial. She was unquestionably beautiful, almost regal.

"Commander Dameron," the woman said. "Do you know who I am?"

Poe nodded. He was acutely aware, now, that his flight suit was soaked with rain and sweat, that he likely smelled like the hind end of a bantha, and that he had disobeyed direct orders that had come down not just from Deso but higher. From as high as Command. From as high as the Senate, perhaps.

He came to attention, snapped a salute, and held it.

"General Organa," he said.

General Leia Organa left her gaze on him for a second more, her expression unchanged, brown eyes seeming sad and weary and strong all at once. Then she waved a hand, dismissing the salute, as if bored by the need for such things.

"At ease. Have a seat, Poe. I'm going to call you Poe, if that's all right."

"Whatever you like, General."

"I like Poe." She moved from behind the desk and hooked one of the nearby chairs with the toe of her boot, pulling it into position before taking a seat. She gestured to the empty chairs, and Poe took one and turned it to face her.

"You should see your expression," General Organa said. She smiled, and that, too, touched her eyes, gave them a warmth that made Poe feel like he was nine again. "I'm not that frightening, surely."

"No, ma'am. Not . . . no, ma'am."

"The problem with a reputation is that it can become a legend." General Organa tugged at the shoulder of her uniform, adjusting it. She shrugged. "Don't be deceived, Poe. I'm not a legend."

Poe grinned and shook his head. "You're not sitting where I'm sitting, General."

"I'm a soldier, Poe. Like you. A soldier with rank and experience, too much experience, perhaps. But just another soldier."

"If you say so, ma'am."

"I do. And stop calling me ma'am."

"Yes, General."

She chuckled. "Oh, it's going to be like that,

is it? All right, *Commander* Dameron. Do you know why you're here?"

Poe shook his head. Three minutes earlier, he'd have been relatively certain of the answer: that he was, at best, about to be knocked down to private and grounded for life.

"Tell me about the *Yissira Zyde*," Leia said. "Everything."

She listened intently, her chin in her hand, her elbow on her knee. Poe couldn't remember ever having felt so *heard* by anyone in all his life. When he talked about the encounter at OR-Kappa-2722 she rose, moved to the maps marking fleet and troop movements, and examined them as she asked him to keep on speaking. She made notations on each map before returning to her seat, and when Poe finished she remained silent for almost a minute, staring past his shoulder at nothing, or perhaps at something only she could see. Memory or the future, Poe didn't know which. Finally, she focused on him again.

"That was exceptionally foolish of you," Leia said. "You barely got out of there with your life."

"In my defense, General, there's no way I

could've known I'd find a First Order staging point."

"But you hoped you would. Or something like it."

"Yes," he said.

"The need to do what's right, and maybe find a little adventure along the way."

Poe shifted in his seat.

"You remind me of my brother," Leia said softly. "Fly like him, too, apparently."

Poe looked at her, surprised and flattered at once. The question pressed him, begged to be asked, but before he could find the courage to voice it, she went on.

"Have you heard of the Resistance, Poe?"

"Rumors, mostly."

"Such as?"

"Such as there's a splinter of the Republic military that . . . that feels the Republic isn't taking certain threats as seriously as they maybe ought to be taking them. Specifically the threat posed by the First Order."

"That's a very diplomatic way to put it, but not an entirely inaccurate one." General Leia Organa exhaled and settled back in her chair, looking him over again. The smile returned, slighter, perhaps sadder. "You've made some people very angry, you know that, Poe? Not letting matters drop when you were told to, disobeying direct orders. Technically, one could argue that you stole a Republic X-wing for personal use."

"I'm a Republic officer, General. I swore an oath to protect the Republic, to—"

She held up a hand. "No, you misunderstand. I like it. It was rash of you, as I said, it was foolish. But we could use some rash these days, and foolish and passionate are often confused, and passion is something we desperately need."

Poe blinked.

"I can whitewash your little trip out to OR-Kappa-2722 for you. I can sweep it under the rug if you like. You can go back to leading Rapier Squadron and having your hands tied by Command, by Major Deso, by politicians who don't recognize what's happening right before their eyes. I can make it all go away, Poe."

She leaned forward.

"Or you can join the Resistance and help us stop the First Order before it's too late."

"Where do I sign up?" Poe asked.

In the end, Karé and Iolo came with him, all that remained of Rapier Squadron taken under the wing of the Resistance, and for the next few months Poe found himself putting in more cockpit time than he had since training, now behind the stick of an older T-70 X-wing. Aside from the early recruiting efforts to find additional pilots, most of it was confined to scouting missions, long-range reconnaissance, searching for signs of First Order movement and positions—an attempt to, as General Organa put it, "find the head of the dragon."

Rapier Squadron was transferred from Mirrin Prime and redeployed aboard a refitted Mon Calamari cruiser called *Echo of Hope*. Poe found himself, while still holding the rank of commander, now in charge of his own fighter wing, with Iolo and Karé both promoted to captain under him, each of them responsible for their own squadrons, Dagger and Stiletto, respectively. Between scouting missions there were briefings, debriefings, and countless meetings, often with General Organa herself, and Ematt, and twice with Admiral Ackbar, whom Leia herself had convinced to come out of retirement.

The Resistance, Poe learned, was small, but among its personnel were some of the most dedicated and motivated people he had ever met, coming from all over the galaxy. Most of the core command staff surrounding General Organa were veterans themselves, many with experience dating back to the Galactic Civil War, and more than once he found himself speaking to someone who had known his parents, who had flown alongside his mother, who had been in the trenches with his father. It was, strangely, like coming home, as if this was the place Poe had been meant to be all along.

But there were many who had never seen Endor or Hoth or any of the countless battles in between. Two of his new squadron—Teffer and Jess, both human—were younger than he and each of them had stories to tell about the First Order that made Poe all the more determined that he had made the right choice. There wasn't one of them in the Resistance who didn't see the First Order for what it was, who didn't believe that its threat was both real and pressing.

Despite that commitment, the Resistance found itself stymied. Republic space and First Order space were separated by a buffer zone of neutral systems, and the peace that had been negotiated—a peace that many, including Poe, believed existed in name only—meant that military action taken by one side upon the other was considered an overt act of war. It didn't seem to matter that evidence of First Order incursions into Republic space continued to mount; the Republic refused to take any action outside of the most formal diplomatic protest. Striking directly at the First Order was out of the question. As Leia explained it to Poe, Resistance action had to remain covert, at least until irrefutable evidence of the First Order's violation of the peace could be presented to Republic Command.

It was this that led to General Organa's recruiting Poe for Operation: Sabre Strike.

"This is Senator Erudo Ro-Kiintor," Leia told Poe. They were alone in her office aboard *Home One*, off of the situation room. "The senior senator from Hevurion to the Republic."

The holo rotated slowly, showing a tall and thin human, entirely bald, wearing a narrow-slitted visor over his eyes. It was a press image, taken at some official function, and to Poe's eyes

Senator Ro-Kiintor looked overdressed and self-important, but that may have been more his personal bias than anything else. He wasn't feeling particularly warm toward members of the Republic Senate these days.

"If you say so, General."

Leia flicked a control on the display, and the image vanished, to be replaced by a similarly rotating schematic, this of a ship. It was sleek, short amidships but broadening away from the keel, with what Poe thought was an unnecessarily ostentatious flaring at the wings.

"This is the *Hevurion Grace*, Senator Ro-Kiintor's personal yacht," Leia said.

Poe nodded slightly. "It's a *Pinnacle*-class luxury ship, made by Vekker Corp. I've seen *Pinnacles* once or twice before. They're exclusive ships, everything aboard handmade, or so Vekker advertises. Only the very wealthy can afford them. They trade luxury for efficiency, practically hang an invitation off the hull for pirates saying, 'Money in here.'"

The general grinned, and when she did her eyes seemed even livelier than ever, that brown warmth in them almost glowing.

"Could you fly one?"

Poe ran a hand through his hair. "Sure. It's designed to be flown by a single pilot, though it crews better with two. Not counting, of course, any servants the owner may want aboard."

"Good," Leia said. "I want you to steal it."

Poe looked from her to the image of the *Hevurion Grace* and back again. He answered her grin with his own. "Sure. Anything else you'd like while I'm at it? Maybe pick you up one of those new Nebulon-Ks?"

"I'm not entirely convinced the Nebulon-Ks have solved their combustion-shielding problems." She switched the display off, and her smile faded, the joke at its end.

"What's this about, General?"

"We've suspected Senator Ro-Kiintor of colluding with the First Order for years, Commander. He's delayed or derailed motions covering everything from sanctions to increased support for the Republic Navy. He's taken numerous unscheduled and impromptu vacations to locations in the buffer region, in the neutral territories. There've been sightings of the *Hevurion Grace* in First Order space. Large sums transferred to his accounts through shells and third-party corporations via the CSA. He's not only in with the First Order, but he's in deep, Poe. He may have access to the top, to General Hux. Perhaps to Snoke."

Leia rubbed a thumb against her temple. "But we haven't been able to prove any of this, Poe. No hard evidence, just circumstantial. And we've tried, believe me. Twice in the last year Ematt's sent his agents aboard the *Hevurion Grace* after one of the senator's trips, trying to access the logs, the navicomputer, to prove where he's been. Each time the files had been purged prior to landing."

"You want me to kidnap a Republic senator?"

She looked alarmed by the suggestion. "No, no, that's precisely what I *don't* want you to do. I want the ship, I want those logs, the navicomputer data, all of it, before anyone's had a chance to cover their tracks, you understand? But no loss of life, not even a bruise on the senator or any of the crew aboard if it can be possibly helped. And it must be completely deniable. Ro-Kiintor is a traitor, I'm sure of it, but until we can prove it, he remains a member of the Senate, and the Resistance will honor that. We *must* honor that, or we're no better than the First Order."

Poe frowned. "If they're purging the data, they're almost certainly doing so within minutes of coming out of hyperspace."

"That's Ematt's thinking, as well."

"It's a very tight window in which to take the ship. And it'll have to be done in space, it can't wait until the senator's landed."

"I am aware of that. I'm aware of exactly how difficult this mission will be. Which is why I'm giving you the option of saying no, Commander. I have to stress this, Poe." Leia reached out, took his hand, and squeezed it. She was meeting his eyes, as grave as he had ever seen her. "This is *not* an order. It could go very, very wrong, and if it does, the Resistance would have to deny any involvement. You and anyone you took with you to do this would be on your own."

She released his hand and sat back. That air of sadness had descended on her once more. His father had carried a similar melancholy after his mother had passed; Poe would see it descend on him like a shadow, settle over his shoulders like a blanket made of warmth and memory and longing and loss. Leia wore something made of the same material, and not for the first time Poe wondered how she had come by it and, perhaps more importantly, who had given it to her.

"I'm going to need a few things," Poe said.

"First of all, this is a volunteer mission," Poe told Iolo and Karé. "You want to take a pass, it will most definitely not be held against you. I will probably think even more highly of you if you say no. It verges on crazy. It is entirely unofficial."

Karé stretched her long legs out in front of her and braced her hands behind her neck as a makeshift headrest. They were in Poe's quarters aboard *Echo of Hope*, late at night ship's time, just the three of them and their droids. Any sense of formality displayed in front of their respective squadrons was entirely absent.

"I love it when he talks like this," Karé told Iolo. "You always know it's going to be something good when he talks like this."

"I'm not sure it's something 'good,'" Iolo said.

"We haven't heard it yet."

"And you won't unless you let me talk," Poe said.

Karé tucked her legs beneath her chair and straightened in her seat. "Sir, yes, sir, Commander, sir!"

Poe laughed, then turned to BB-8, and the droid took that as his cue to begin projecting the visuals for the briefing from his central lens. The images floated in front of all three pilots, flickering occasionally: the schematics of the *Hevurion Grace* and the file information on its crew and passengers, including Senator Ro-Kiintor. Karé laughed when she realized who they were looking at, and Iolo's already slightly larger eyes grew even larger. But neither of them objected, both listening carefully as Poe broke down the operation, the objective, and his plan.

"It's a tight window," Poe said. "We have to hit the ship the moment it comes out of hyperspace, we have to disable it, get me aboard, get the senator and anyone else on the ship into the escape pods and off the vessel, restart the engines, and then get out of there again. And we have to do it within eight minutes."

"Why eight minutes?" Iolo asked.

"Republic response time to the Uvoss system," Karé said, and Poe nodded. "It's not on any of the patrol routes and that's probably why the senator's been using it as his hyperspace entry and exit when he's taking these little jaunts."

"But the first thing they'll do when they real-ize they're under attack is send out a distress call," Poe said. "Nearest Republic squadron will need at least eight minutes to respond."

"So we need to be gone by the time they get there," Iolo said.

"Exactly," said Poe.

"At least eight minutes?"

"Minimum. Could take them longer."

"Then let's hope it takes them longer," Iolo said.

Since the mission required deniability, none of them could use Resistance-affiliated vessels. They had to leave their X-wings behind. Through some wheeling and dealing and the judicious use of favors owed to him, Poe managed to acquire three venerable Incom Z-95 Headhunters for the operation. The fighters had entered produc-tion during the Clone Wars and were, in many ways, considered the precursor to the X-wing class. Long retired from official military use, the Z-95s had since dispersed throughout the gal-axy, finding homes with smugglers, gangsters, pirates, and any others who wanted a fighter to do their business, legitimate or otherwise. If things went horribly wrong, at least Poe, Karé, and Iolo couldn't be accused of using Republic, or Resistance, resources for their rogue operation.

Complicating things further, none of the Z-95s were fitted for astromech assist, which meant that all of their hyperspace jumps to and from the Uvoss system, where they intended to intercept the *Hevurion Grace*, needed to be preprogrammed. There was an upside to this, in that it meant Karé and Iolo could shave a handful of seconds off of their escape; Poe would have to rely on a data chip carried with him to force-feed the jump coordinates to the *Hevurion Grace*'s navi-computer once he had control of the cockpit.

BB-8 did not like the idea of being left behind, and made his displeasure known to Poe.

"I'm going to be sitting in a Z-95 cockpit wearing an EVA suit," Poe told the droid. "And you want to sit on my lap? Worry less about being left behind and more about making certain the concussion missiles are fitted with the proper warheads, okay, buddy?"

The droid did as asked, but Poe had the unmistakable sense that BB-8 was sulking. There was no other word for it.

"I'm going to come back," Poe said. "I always do."

They'd been on station for just under seven hours, floating in the cold silence of the Uvoss system. The reason the Republic had no patrols in the area was evident. Of the three planets in the system, two were gas giants so enormous they'd barely missed out on becoming stars in their own right, massive enough that their gravity wells created a distinct, if minor, hazard for hyperspace travel. The third planet was, charitably, a bulbous chunk of iron that whirred in an ever-tightening orbit around the Uvoss sun, itself an unremarkable standard yellow star. Given a couple of thousand more years, the planet rock would be turned into a light snack for the star.

That was it; there was nothing else. Just the silence, the cold, and the need to be patient. Poe, Karé, and Iolo couldn't even speak to one another, forced to maintain radio silence. Even for Poe, who had long before come to terms with the boredom of space travel and the patience required to combat it, the wait was particularly grueling. The Z-95 cockpit was small to begin with—Karé had complained endlessly about the lack of legroom—but with the addition of the EVA suit Poe was wearing, there was almost no room to move at all. To save time, he'd sealed the suit on takeoff, which meant he was entirely enclosed, helmet and all. While still aboard the fighter he could connect to the ship's environmental controls via a hose in the side of the space suit, but the air he was breathing had long before begun to taste like stale sweat and plastic. Poe had never in all his life wanted so much to brush his teeth.

It occurred to him that he, Karé, and Iolo were going to do to the *Hevurion Grace* exactly what the First Order had done to the *Yissira Zyde*.

It's one thing to be bored and patient. It's another thing to be bored, patient, and have to remain alert, and that was truly the hardest part of it all. The pilots floated, each alone with their thoughts, fighting the inevitable drowsiness, struggling to keep one eye on where they expected Senator Ro-Kiintor to burst back into realspace and the other on their controls. Poe grew so bored, he actually began to count how many yawns he'd stifled.

Then Iolo's engines pulsed, powering up, and Poe knew that the Keshian had seen with his specialized vision what Poe and Karé couldn't. A ripple in the fabric of realspace perhaps, or a swell in the UV or infrared spectrum. Poe forced his heavily gloved thumb down on the activator and wrapped his other hand, just as heavily gauntleted, around the yoke and felt his Z-95 come back to life just as the *Hevurion Grace* seemed to stretch into reality from nothingness. The ship wasn't there, and then it was, and all at once Iolo and Karé were hurtling forward in the darkness and Poe was on their tails, following their attack.

It went perfectly at first.

Predictably, the *Hevurion Grace* broadcast its distress signal even as it attempted to come about, and in response Poe keyed a control on the arm of his suit. An illuminated timer popped into view inside his helmet, easily readable from the corner of one eye, counting down from eight minutes.

The clock was now running.

Iolo launched first, two modified concussion missiles that streaked toward the yacht, Karé's chasing after them. The *Hevurion Grace* tried to roll into an evasive maneuver, managed even to launch its countermeasures, a burst of flares designed to force the incoming missiles to explode prematurely, but despite its best efforts, two got through. The first impacted high on the yacht's stern, the second detonating on proximity, perhaps a kilometer off the bow. Bolts of energy exploded and blue tendrils raced over the hull of the ship, dancing and sparking, flowing into every seam of the vessel.

The *Hevurion Grace* went dead in space, power flickering out as the ionization took hold of its controls.

Poe throttled up, his fighter slipping between Karé's and Iolo's as each peeled off, starboard and port. He keyed the autopilot, the nose of the fighter now pointed some dozen meters beneath the belly of the yacht, in line with the looming gas giant beyond it. He fumbled with the quick release on his chest, his fingers clumsy in the oversized gloves, the timer still counting down with just over seven and a half minutes left. *Hevurion Grace* was coming quickly closer. The harness broke apart around him, and Poe slammed his left fist on the ejector plate, snapping it open and taking hold of the handle. He wrenched it and even through the helmet heard the screams of the ship's alarms, questioning the wisdom of leaving the fighter at this point in time, in this place, at this speed. He yanked again and the explosive bolts on the canopy detonated, sending it up and over the tail of the Z-95, and almost as quickly Poe felt himself slipping free from the flight couch, weightless and untethered, as the micro-repulsorlift field spat him out of the fighter.

Then he was in space, still being carried forward by the momentum of the Z-95, still hurtling toward the *Hevurion Grace* far, far too quickly. At this speed, a collision with the hull of the yacht would be fatal, would turn Poe to a smear of jelly inside the EVA suit. Beneath his feet, he could see the Z-95 keeping pace, an optical illusion that made it seem that both he and the fighter were motionless, that it was the yacht approaching them, rather than the other way around. The range finder in the HUD of his helmet was counting down the distance rapidly, faster than the clock inexorably running down.

Poe waited for as long as he could, longer than he should've, before activating the maneuver jets on the space suit, a full-burst deceleration firing from the chest piece, boots, and helmet at once. The yacht was still approaching fast, and he had a moment of near panic when he thought the maneuver wouldn't work at all, and then he glanced down and the Z-95 had vanished, and when he raised his eyes he could see the glow of its engines, already past the *Hevurion Grace* and disappearing toward the gas giant. The fighter would never reach the surface, crushed into its components by the tremendous pressure of the planet's atmosphere.

Poe slammed into the yacht hard enough that his head snapped forward in his helmet, hard enough that he felt the impact run through his body, hard enough that his breath exploded out of him, made a film of condensation on the inside of his visor. He tasted blood, scrabbled for a handhold, and finding one began pulling himself, hand over hand, along the hull of the yacht. His head was ringing, and he felt disembodied, and it wasn't until his vision had cleared that he realized he'd managed to reach the access port and was already using the fusion torch from his belt to break the seals.

The timer was down to six minutes, forty-seven seconds.

One of the Z-95s crossed his vision, Iolo visible for an instant as he rocked the fighter, waving with its wings. Karé crossed in the other direction, each of them now flying a limited patrol around the vessel.

The last seal popped, the hatch parting enough for Poe to get his gloved hands into the opening. He was fighting his own weightlessness as much as the yacht, and even with his gloves and boots magnetized to the hull there was a limit to how much strength he could exert. He pushed and pulled, and the timer was down to six minutes and three seconds before he managed to force the opening wide enough to squeeze himself inside. He lost another seventeen seconds resealing it behind him. With the power disabled on the yacht, the gravity emulators had gone offline, as well, and he had to pull himself hand over hand down the ladder and into the ship itself, the path illuminated only by the floodlight on his helmet.

He'd just hit the bottom when the lights, and the gravity, came back, and Poe spared an instant to thank whoever or whatever it was that watched out for reckless, foolish pilots. A few seconds earlier, he'd have landed headfirst on the deck and possibly broken his neck.

Poe righted himself, reached around to his back, and freed the blaster carbine strapped there. He slapped the door release, raised the weapon to his shoulder, and switched on the speakers on his suit as he stepped forward.

"This vessel is now the property of the Irving Boys!" The speakers distorted Poe's voice, made it seem more droid than human, amplified and reverberating.

It got the desired result.

Three beings stood in the hall when Poe emerged, one of them presumably the pilot judging by how he was dressed, another a servant, and Senator Ro-Kiintor himself. All turned and stared at Poe, hidden in his space suit, taken utterly by surprise by the boarding. They gaped at him, motionless, and Poe could only imagine what they were seeing, this oversized figure in his bulky EVA suit, face hidden behind the tinted visor of his helmet, the blaster carbine in his hands looking comically small.

The senator spluttered. "Do you know who I am? How dare—"

Poe fired a shot at the deck, sending sparks into the air.

"Mine!" Poe roared. "You're good stock! You'll make a fine slave!"

The senator blanched, recoiling to hide behind his servant.

"Now . . . now let's not do anything hasty. . . ."

"You have ten seconds to leave my ship!" Poe said. "Or else you'll be mine, too!"

He fired a second shot into the deck for emphasis.

The senator, the pilot, and the servant practically trampled one another running for the escape pods.

With three minutes and twenty-nine seconds left on the timer, everything went wrong.

Poe was in the cockpit, helmet and gloves now unceremoniously dumped on the floor, the data chip with the hyperspace coordinates plugged into the navicomputer. He was working on restarting the *Hevurion Grace*'s main engines when Iolo's voice came over the comm.

"Uh-oh."

Just that, and it was enough for Poe to snap his

head up from his work and search the empty space beyond the cockpit canopy. It was just possible— barely possible—that they'd miscalculated and the Republic had managed a speedier response than anticipated. But even as he thought that, Poe knew he was wrong. Iolo's Keshian eyes had seen trouble coming, but not soon enough to do anything about it, and what had been an empty view suddenly filled with one ship, then another, then another as vessels snapped back into realspace.

"First Order!" Poe shouted into his comm. "Jump! Iolo, Karé, get out of here!"

TIEs were already launching from the belly of the two Star Destroyers that had appeared, one of them a new model *Resurgent* class. Another flight dropped from its moorings alongside the Nebulon-K that had come with them. Smaller vessels, assault ships, popped into view. Proximity alarms on the *Hevurion Grace* began screaming, and Poe twisted around, slapping switches back into silence.

"Commander, what's your time to jump?" Karé asked.

"I gave you an order, Captain Kun."

"Sorry, can't hear you because of all these *TIE fighters* coming at me."

Poe glanced at the charging monitor for the hyperdrive. The ion blast to the yacht had forced almost every system aboard into reset, and while the navicomputer now had coordinates for his jump locked, it was the drive itself that needed to restart. Unfamiliar though he was with the flight controls of a *Pinnacle*-class yacht, Poe could see it would be another ninety seconds on the outside before the ship's twin SoroSuub Hawke engines reached full power. Any attempt to jump prior to that would be pointless; the *Hevurion Grace*'s hyperdrive motivator simply would refuse to engage the engines.

"It's gonna be about forty, forty-five seconds," Poe said. "I can evade these slugs for that long."

"So about a minute and a half," Iolo said. His tone was resigned. "You're a bad liar, Commander."

"I am not." Poe was indignant.

"We'll keep them off your back, Commander." This was Karé again. "You make your back hard for them to climb onto to begin with."

"You're both disobeying my orders." Even as he was saying it, Poe was kicking up the thrust on the yacht's ion engines. At least *those* were fully functional. "Don't think I'll forget this."

"You can court-martial us later, sir," Karé said.

It didn't take long for Poe to realize how serious the First Order was about stopping the *Hevurion Grace*. The first flight of TIEs, eighteen of them, blew straight past Iolo and Karé in their Z-95s without pause or deviation, racing directly for Poe and the yacht. The two leading TIEs had opened fire even before they were in range. Poe concluded three things from this: first, that whoever was flying those TIEs had more enthusiasm than sense; second, that whatever information the Resistance might discover in the yacht's computers was likely to be worth its weight in gold; and third, as a result of the second fact, the First Order was *very* serious about keeping him from escaping.

But that single-mindedness cost them.

For all its reputation as a pure luxury craft, Poe found the yacht surprisingly nimble in his hands, the ship leaping forward with a burst of speed as he opened the thrusters and banked hard, making for the nearest of the Uvoss gas giants. His goal was to put as much space as possible between himself and the capital ships; and the capital ships, he'd noted at once, were closing on him, albeit much more slowly than the TIEs. The TIEs he felt he could handle; the yacht's deflectors were fully charged, and Poe was confident enough in his piloting and, more, in Iolo and Karé that he believed he could survive long enough to make the jump. But those capital ships were another matter, their firepower truly terrifying; a direct hit from any of their turbolaser batteries would turn *Hevurion Grace* into vapor, and Poe Dameron with it.

So the gas giant was really his only choice, and if he could get close enough, there might even be a tactical advantage to be found in the planet's intense gravity. That was the plan, but flying in a straight line would let the TIEs cut him to pieces, and that meant he was jinking, dodging, twisting the yacht in ways he was certain its owner would've wept to witness.

The TIEs were on him as soon as he completed the turn, beginning his run for the gas giant, and *that* was their mistake. Iolo and Karé brought their Z-95s into tight, combat-Corellian turns, coming into line on the tails of the First

Order fighters. In the space of twenty seconds, Poe's comrades had cut the initial force of eighteen down to nine before the remaining TIEs broke off their pursuit, for the moment more concerned with staying alive. Karé bagged another two on the breakaway, and Iolo took out one more.

"Leave some for the rest of us," Poe said.

"You snooze, you lose," Karé said. "Time until jump? For real, please, Commander."

Poe checked the charge meter, did the math quickly in his head. "Another forty seconds."

A turbolaser blast seared space in front of him, the shot so close and so bright that Poe actually flinched. An instant later the yacht bucked, rocking as blasts from two strafing TIEs cut across the top of the hull. Lights lit up across the console, warning him about everything from diminishing deflector shield charge to fastening his safety harness.

"Little help," Poe said.

"On 'em," Iolo said, and an instant later he saw the edge of a Z-95's wing flash over the cockpit, and the bright glow of a TIE's destruction.

"That *Resurgent* class is closing fast," Karé said.

"You guys need to go, now," Poe said.

"Right after you do."

Poe bit back a curse. The Star Destroyer in question was a beast, capable of delivering a withering assault with its heavy cannons and anti-starship batteries. In a straight line, running at full speed, it could be faster even than the TIEs it seemed to spit out in endless waves, powered as it was by multiple and massive ion drives designed to propel its bulk through space. It was a staggering amount of thrust. The trade was, of course, that running in a straight line and at full speed meant an equally staggering amount of counter-thrust was required to execute even the slightest maneuver, the barest change of direction. The Star Destroyers were big, and they were powerful, but only the most reckless of commanders would employ their speed and sacrifice their maneuverability.

He had to make a choice, Poe realized. He could continue racing for the gas giant in the hope that the massive planet's gravity would scare the capital ships off, or . . .

"Head for that *Resurgent* class," Poe said.

"Say what now?" Karé asked.

"One hit from those turbolasers and we're done," Iolo said.

"And one hit from those turbolasers, those TIEs are done, too."

"That close, you're vulnerable to their tractor beams—"

"*Resurgent* beam emitters are to the prow." Poe was already rebalancing the yacht's thrusters, wheeling the ship into yet another corkscrew turn and reversing direction. "Don't come at it from the front."

"Oh, well, that settles that," Karé said. "Sure, let's charge the Star Destroyer. Why not? Coming, Iolo?"

"Do I have a choice?"

"No," Poe said.

The two Z-95s came in on his starboard wing, then staggered back. The second wave of TIEs was still a fair distance out, but that wouldn't last for long. Poe glanced out the canopy and saw white mist wafting from the middle of one of the Z-95's wings, along with an occasional spark of electricity.

"Iolo, check your port side."

"Yeah, I know," Iolo said. "Not really much I can do about it right now, though."

"You could leave," Poe said.

"What, and miss this? Karé would never let me hear the end of it."

"That is true," Karé said.

"Break," Poe said.

They all knew the maneuver and executed it so quickly that the three ships were moving apart almost before Poe had finished speaking the word. In the lead, Poe took the yacht high, climbing and spinning, while Karé snapped her Z-95 to port beneath him and Iolo put his own fighter into a twisting dive. The TIEs opened up a fraction of a moment later, their shots lancing past harmlessly, then split their formation, and Poe guessed at least half of them were coming for *Hevurion Grace*.

The *Resurgent* class was drawing closer. A turbolaser blast detonated perhaps only a half kilometer in front of Poe, and he felt the yacht shiver as he sped through the dissipating energy an instant later. He was, despite his own advice, approaching the prow, with TIEs closing in from his right and behind. The ship bucked and shuddered as one of the chasing fighters sent blaster bolts glancing off the yacht. The shields flickered, but held.

The *Hevurion Grace* had never been built for combat, but that didn't mean it was defenseless. It boasted a single dual-cannon turret, mounted on its dorsal side, near the tail.

Poe noted that it was fully automated.

He put the yacht into a sharp wingover and bled off some of his speed while reorienting away from the bow of the *Resurgent* class, now looming before him. The move brought two of the TIEs in close, and Poe could imagine those pilots in their flight suits, thumbs itching on their triggers, lining up their shots, and then he hit the actuator on the turret and felt more than heard the gun opening fire. The salvo cut the two nearest TIEs to pieces and clipped two more that had been following close behind. The pursuers banked away, trying to reacquire a new attack angle on *Hevurion Grace*.

Poe could hear Iolo and Karé's chatter over the comms, rapid-fire give and take, the two of them working in concert. Another TIE down, and another, but for every one that Iolo or Karé managed to take down, there seemed another to take its place.

"Iolo! Watch it!"

"I've got no room!"

"Cut port, cut port, I'll pick him up!"

Static burst across the comm and fizzled, fol-lowed by a fraction of a second's silence that felt much, much longer.

Then Iolo's voice: "—hit, been hit, losing power—"

"Iolo, jump," Poe said. The *Resurgent* class was a blur outside his cockpit as he spiraled and pulled up, reversing again for the command tower. "Go!"

"Not going to leave you!"

The turbolasers from the *Resurgent* class were firing almost constantly. The yacht rocked again as the *Hevurion Grace* hit the wake of another deto-nation, this to the stern. One of the ion thrusters flickered, then dumped its charge, and at the same moment the hyperdrive motivator announced it was now prepared to initiate the jump to light-speed. Another blast detonated so close to the cockpit Poe feared the canopy would shatter.

"We're leaving together," Poe said. "Break off and jump to lightspeed!"

He yanked back on the yoke hard enough that the yacht's gravity emulators snapped his head against the seat. The *Resurgent* class went from beneath him and ahead to somehow below and behind, and he was climbing fast, spinning in the ascent, and he could see the Z-95s, if only for an instant, similarly trying to turn onto their jump vectors. Now that their target was away from the Star Destroyer, the TIEs were once again in pursuit, their incoming fire blurring with the resumption of turbolaser barrages.

"Jump! Go!"

Karé's fighter went first, stretched and then vanished, and Iolo's followed, and Poe reached for the jump initiator, pulled it smoothly back, and *Hevurion Grace* rumbled all around him. Then the TIEs and the frigate and the Star Destroyers and everything of Uvoss vanished, replaced by the hypnotizing swirl of the hyperspace tunnel.

Iolo and Karé were in the hangar bay waiting for him when Poe landed aboard *Echo of Hope*. They watched as he dropped the main ramp and descended, and for a moment all three pilots just looked at each other. Then Karé burst into laughter and threw her arms around him and Iolo was clapping him on the back and all of them were talking at once about how *that* had been flying and Iolo had gotten lucky and Karé had saved him and he had saved her and they'd lost count of how many times they'd had each other's backs. Laughing at the thought of the First Order trying to explain to General Hux or whoever exactly how they'd managed to be vexed by three pilots flying a luxury yacht and two archaic Z-95s and—

"Muran would've loved to have seen that," Iolo said.

That brought them back into silence for a moment, all three of them remembering their absent friend.

"He'd have been proud," Karé said.

"Yes," Poe said. "Yes, he would've been."

Between Iolo and Karé, Poe could see General Organa at the entrance of the bay, the protocol droid that so often accompanied her at her side. She caught his eye and Poe nodded and put a hand on Iolo and Karé's shoulders.

"Go get cleaned up," Poe said. "We'll have a toast to Muran."

Leia waited until they were gone before approaching Poe. "Threepio, go aboard please and see what you can get from the flight computers."

"Of course, Princess Leia," the droid said. He nodded to Poe in a stilted approximation of a human acknowledgement, then made his way up the ramp.

Leia was looking up at Poe, smiling ever so slightly. "Flyboys. You're all the same."

"Some of us are flygirls," Poe said.

"Captain Kun is an exceptional pilot, without question, as is Captain Arana, for that matter. But it's a rare pilot who engages one frigate and two Star Destroyers and lives to tell the tale."

"Word travels fast."

"Yes," Leia said. "It does."

"Princess Leia?" the protocol droid called from the top of the ramp. "I think perhaps you better see this."

"It's never anything good when he says that," Leia told Poe.

It was the next morning, before Poe had even managed to make it to breakfast when he learned how right she was.

He'd had difficulty sleeping, the elation of the mission's success fading as the hours had length-ened into night, his mind turning to dark and, frankly, depressing thoughts. When he finally did manage to sleep, it was restless and unsatisfying, and when he awoke it was with the sense that he'd had no rest at all.

As soon as Poe switched the lights on in his quarters BB-8 rolled forward, chirping softly and directing Poe's attention to the blinking message light on his console. It was from the general, asking that he come and see her right away. He took her literally, dressed without bothering to run through the refresher and made his way through the corridor to her office.

General Organa met him at the door and shut it behind him. Her movements were deliberate and slow, as if she was lost in thought, her manner markedly subdued compared to the day before, as if she was wrestling with some dilemma deep within herself. She pointed Poe to one of the chairs but didn't sit herself, instead pacing the length of the room for several seconds, her chin against her chest, her brow furrowed.

"How are you feeling?" she asked abruptly. She was staring at him.

"I'm . . . I'm fine, General."

She arched an eyebrow. "I'll rephrase. *What* are you feeling?"

He wondered if it was on his face, the thoughts

that had kept him up half the night. He wondered, for a moment, if her night hadn't been similarly rough.

"I'm angry," Poe admitted. "And I'm worried, General. A member of the Republic Senate was in so deep with the First Order that when he put out a distress call *they* came to try and rescue him, and when they did it, they pulled out all the stops. Two Star Destroyers and I couldn't count how many TIEs, and maybe they knew he was no longer aboard but maybe they didn't, but they wanted *Hevurion Grace* destroyed. They were willing to kill their man to keep us from taking that vessel."

He paused, cautious that he'd said too much, perhaps, but Leia was listening to him exactly as she had back on Mirrin Prime, and after a second he continued.

"I keep thinking, this man, Ro-Kiintor, he's a *senator*. He's in the heart of the Republic, *our* Republic. And he was a traitor. And I'm wondering how many more are just like him, how many more are working for the First Order, how many more have sold us out."

"Yet you still believe in the Republic, Poe."

"Absolutely, yes." Poe spoke without hesitation. "I remember how my parents spoke about life under the Empire, General. The fear, they said it was like a cloud everywhere you went, that it was so thick you could . . . you could breathe it. They used to say, until the Rebellion . . . they said you could see hopelessness in the eyes of everyone you met."

"That's the word," Leia said, as much to herself as to Poe. "Without hope."

"Where did it go?" he asked, and the question seemed so much more important than he meant it to be, but as he asked he was thinking of his father, and his mother, of everything they had sacrificed and fought for. Thinking of Leia Organa, one of the last survivors of Alderaan standing before him—of everything she had lost, both what Poe knew and what was rumored.

"I don't know," she said. "But I know we have to find it again."

She drew herself up, her shoulders squaring, her jaw setting, the determination she was known for once again fully apparent. Whatever her internal debate, she had reached a conclusion. Poe watched her turn to her desk and key a sequence into the small safe built in its side. A drawer popped open, and her hand went in, then emerged with a data chip, slender and blue tinted.

"We obtained a lot of information from the computers aboard *Hevurion Grace*," Leia said, looking at the chip. "A wealth of information. But there was something else, something that . . . others may have missed. A piece of a puzzle I've been working for . . . for a long time to solve."

She set the data chip in Poe's palm.

"I think the First Order is trying to solve it, too, Poe. We have to solve it first. We have to find *him* first."

"Who?"

"His name is Lor San Tekka."

"Lor San Tekka," Poe repeated. "Why's the First Order so desperate to find him?"

"They think he knows something. I'm hoping he does, too." Leia took his hand and folded his fingers closed over the data chip. She met his eyes. "I'm hoping Lor San Tekka knows where to find my brother, Poe. And Luke Skywalker may be the only hope we have left."